The Chameleon Room

Kerry Hadley

authorHOUSE®

AuthorHouse™ UK Ltd.
500 Avebury Boulevard
Central Milton Keynes, MK9 2BE
www.authorhouse.co.uk
Phone: 08001974150

First published by AuthorHouse   11/21/2008

ISBN: 978-1-4389-2271-3 (sc)

Printed in the United States of America
Bloomington, Indiana

This book is printed on acid-free paper.

The Chameleon Room

I

It had been raining and the light was beginning to fail behind the sad looking deciduous trees whose aging leaves were deserting them. The impression was one of brownness, of dourness, of cold. Out of the corner of my eye I saw a figure, small and naked. Falling. Falling from the muddy river bank. What must have been a split second shot. Very white skin, almost torpedo shaped body, stubby feet seemingly clamped together at the ankle and arms raised high above the dome-like, hairless head. Not a graceful pose, more like a child's drawing of a fat ballerina. But instantly recognisable. I knew she would be here. Those reluctant links between us were impossible to break.

My automatic reaction was to run, run towards her, and as the wooden bridge rattled beneath my clumsy feet – I'm no athlete and quickly found exhalation almost impossible – I swear our eyes met. Then she was just swallowed up by the river. Moss on the damp ground made me slip a little, but I was determined to get to her. There was a moment as I managed to pick up speed when she appeared to bob up to the surface. Nature is a wonderful thing isn't it? Nature, I thought, would help me save her. Reaching the water's edge – even now I don't know how long it took – I was sure I could still see circular swirls of grey water, like a target, where she was. And bubbles.

I ran, slowed by mud and weeds, like a child into the sea, legs uncontrollable, feeling nothing but a raging desire to reach her, to hold her to me, to be responsible for saving her. A shwump of river water in my ears. A gulp of greasiness. A desperation felt only by the untutored or immature. And there she was again. An arm or a leg. I lurched under the biting cold water, seeing life as a blurred Monet picture. Slow motion. I caught sight of her just as I realised oxygen was becoming a necessity. Lungs burning, head already becoming euphorically light, limbs beginning to seize up, through the murk and particles, I saw her face. She had the expression that she wore when she was busy or concentrating hard, or when she was reprimanding me. Her eyes, translucent, glassy, were not her eyes, they were the eyes of a mad woman and they weren't looking for help. Her sinewy neck strained against the water pressure. She didn't seem to see me in the gloom, though maybe she wasn't looking for me; now I realise it's sometimes only the expected that we choose to see, if you know what I mean. So she probably physically felt my clumsy attempts to save her before any of her other senses computed the situation. And she struggled. She struggled like the mackerel we had caught off the Devon coast a few years earlier; pudgy hands grasping at me and flabby legs kicking me away with unexpected guile. Bubbles left her open mouth in a defiant, straight, even line and I craved the air she rejected. Sinking deeper into the water and in sudden anger at every vile remark she had ever made to me, at every comment she had ever passed about me, at every spiteful thing she had ever done to me, at what she was doing now, I grabbed her ears with my bloodless hands and thrust my mouth to hers, pushing the air from my own lungs into her body. And her glazed eyes gawped at me, cross eyed and expressionless in an effort to focus I suppose. Then, don't ask me how, she shoved me with the full weight of her body so that my lips snapped from hers and we were propelled in opposite directions, away from each other; she downwards further into the darkness and me towards the surface of the water. Her body sank deeper, covered in minute oxygen bubbles – an ingredient of life itself – and yet she was unable and unwilling to take it. Further and further away, she seemed to be waving a kind of grotesque goodbye with her chubby hands, but through the distortion of the water, her face, her skin, her bald, smooth head looked suddenly beautiful to me. At last, she was perfect.

At the surface the air hit me immediately and I languished for a second in life itself, then plummeted into an emotional turmoil, imagining what Angelo would say, imagining a life suffused with blame, feeling my lungs reviving, feeling the guilty water in my ears, eyes, nose; tasting sourness rising from my throat. Crying out, then screaming uselessly "Kary!"

* * * * *

My clothes smelt of shit. My hair hung like damp cardboard and bounced ignominiously off my shoulders. Something cold ran down my legs and arms and face. One foot in front of the other was walking. It didn't feel like walking, but it was. I had lost my shoes and my feet were painfully bare against the hard, dusty pavement. Every now and then a sharp pang of pain rose from the sole of a foot making me hop an obscure dance, away from the pain. Darkness had fallen quickly and I was grateful. My lips were sore and I licked them with a spiky tongue, tasting that bitter, salty taste of the river. I stifled back a sob, remembering my failure, and realised that a man walking a dog across the road was watching me with more than just a passing interest so that when I met his gaze, he did not look away. Who would look away first? His face was vaguely questioning, and now I think about it, I must have looked a mess – damp, bare foot and sobbing. Who wouldn't acknowledge me? I held his gaze for as long as I could and then started to trot in a lumbering, round shouldered, pathetic kind of way, clenching my fists and digging my soft, river-water damaged finger nails into my palms in an effort to motivate myself. A car rounded the corner and I could hear the rap music spill outside, catching a fleeting glance of the baseball capped driver, mouthing the inane words to the song. White tee shirt, roaring engine, then gone. I wondered which was reality, his or mine.

A street light pinged on and fizzed, orange and unnatural above my head, making everything appear artificial, constructed, almost dream-like. I forced my paranoia to feed off the atmosphere and kept running, amazed that I was not yet out of breath, counting breaths and paces, remembering some distant advice about avoiding "stitch", convincing myself that I would run all the way home. The flashing lights of the Paphos Greek Bar raged dimly and my bare feet skimmed dangerously on the pavement outside on the spilt beer and ancient vomit. Sounds of clinking glass, manic laughter and 80's disco music flashed abruptly at me. A waft of cigarette smoke and fried food drifted into me from the open door. I felt sick. And that dreamlike feeling of being held back by an invisible force against my will took hold of me. I kept running and didn't stop until I arrived at home. There, less wet now, I charged upstairs, threw back the duvet and jumped fully clothed into bed, covering myself quickly, being aware only of my regular, thumping heartbeat and stilted breathing against the musty polyester. Darkness was a comfort as I drifted into a fitful sleep.

II

_____

I once walked into an open bathroom door, by accident of course – wasn't looking where I was going or it was dark or something. Kary had left the door open, by accident, she said, and the sharp corner of the door made significant contact with my forehead. An exquisite pain immediately shot through my face and resulted in a vertical purple bruise running from my widow's peak to the bridge of my nose. Angelo said "My god, have you had a tattoo?" and he gazed steadily at my forehead. At first I didn't think the question merited an answer, so looked blankly at him.

Angelo was undoubtedly beautiful. He was sitting in an old brown horsehair armchair amidst a background of sound from the tv. An advertisement for a mobile phone network unsuccessfully demanded our attention and a series of techno images flashed irritatingly into the room. Angelo looked like he could be part of it. His legs were uncrossed with each foot placed firmly on the ground, knees pointed outward so that his denim covered crotch area was exposed. His flat abdomen was hardly obscured by a white cotton tee shirt but his regular breathing ensured that I could make out the undulations in his musculature and my eyes rested momentarily amongst the power such socially accepted perfection created. His hands were resting on the arms of the chair, chalky with unblemished skin and pretty pink finger nails. His long tapered fingers draped idly over the piped edges so that he looked convincingly alert to imminent danger – ready to spring into action. His neck was smooth but for a visible pulsation in a vein or artery and his head was tilted upwards towards me so that the dark prickles on his chin and upper lip were accentuated by the ebbing light in the room. There was a turquoise about his eyes that made me search them for something that just wasn't there. The severe cut of his jaw was almost too contrived and the kick of his blond hair framed a facial symmetry which could, at the very least, cultivate a gaze from onlookers and at most, a drive to deflower, to exploit, to abuse.

The tv droned a repetitive ringtone followed by a silence and I was overtaken by a desire to kiss him, but we were both frozen in the moment – though with hindsight, he was probably just incredulously waiting for my response; a thoroughly meaningless question required a thoroughly meaningless answer. After a while I said "I walked into the door." This seemed to placate the situation and the tension immediately subsided. Angelo's face broke into a grin. "Plonker," he said, shaking his perfect head and, shifting in his chair, turned to watch the tv screen.

The wave of affection I felt for Angelo at that point was palpable and I could not contain the urge to slide onto his lap, throw my arms around his sculpted neck and kiss him wetly on the cheek. His surprise at both my weight on his and the warmth of my kiss formed a natural punctuation mark and he turned his head abruptly so that our eyes were as close as eyes can be without belonging to the same person.

"You're mad!" he whispered.

"Is that the best you can do?" I laughed, clasping his face with both hands and planting a large-lipped kiss on his mouth. His lips felt big and smooth, warm and red and the strength of his arms around my waist, pulling me towards him surprised me so that my own mouth mirrored his in a stretched smiley crescent, teeth clinking and silly expulsions emerging as sniggers.

An icy voice from behind me, unmistakeably Kary's, announced flatly, "I'm home."

A feeling of being caught out inexplicably overwhelmed me, and I felt my face redden. Kary stood grimly in the doorway and I was struck by how the light from behind her made her outline look like a penguin. It was hard to see her facial expression but the sound of her laboured nasal breathing, so loud it was audible above the sound of the tv, was signifier enough of her mood. For a moment she didn't move at all, and then without warning, she disappeared towards the kitchen. Angelo's face was still very close to mine and when I turned my head towards him, our noses clipped making him laugh just a little too loud. I didn't laugh. I knew this would be unwise with Kary still in earshot, and I rolled off Angelo's lap and sidled into the kitchen. Kary's back was towards me, she appeared to be busy doing something at the sink. And she was muttering. There were two choices when Kary was in this frame of mind: ignore the mood she was in by leaving her to it or ignore the mood she was in by chatting to her as if she was fine. That day I chose the latter.

"Hi Kary," I was standing beside her now, looking at her strange rounded profile. Her hands were busy doing something in a sink full of washing up water. I could see her general mood was bordering on angry, but decided to continue with a conversation. Kary in a bad mood was never very pleasant and anything I could do to pull her out of it seemed sensible.

"Had a good day?" My regret at this particular question was instant. Now I think back, I wonder why I really asked. She clearly had not had a good day, and the mere asking of the question would only ignite any problems further, and anyway, what could I do about them? Nevertheless, as humans, I guess we have our reasons for communicating, and in this case, my reason was to provoke a conversation, any conversation, so that at least some sense of "normality" could exist in our house. Without Kary's positive involvement, our home seemed not worth living in. Her mood coloured the place. She dominated the atmosphere and was capable of making it wonderful and dreadful in equal parts. In some ways, asking this question implied that I cared that she had had a good day. As it happened, I did, because if her day had been good, I could relax a little. I knew, of course, that her seeing me with Angelo would have tainted any good day for her, but I figured I could counter balance that by ignoring him now and giving Kary all my attention. That was how it was in our house. A house of strategic moves which sometimes worked and sometimes didn't. An imbalanced house, one that was fragile and uncomfortable, but one in which we all played an equally important role in its discomfort. Now, of course, it is clear to me why this was the case, but at the time, we were all as blind as each other. As it happened, I needn't have worried about my style of questioning because Kary continued kneading something in the washing up water, staring with increasing irritation at the mounting bubbles.

"We were just watching tv." This sometimes worked: taking her mind off her own egocentrism by focussing on my own.

"Load of rubbish," I continued inanely, "too many adverts these days. Spoils the programme I think. We should get Sky or Cable, then we'd have more choice. There are some really good film channels and it doesn't cost much. What do you think?"

Kary's arms, now thoroughly covered in unnaturally white bubbles, continued to toil away and even though she did not answer me, I knew her well enough to know that she wanted to. She was holding back. I could tell because her thin lips were even thinner for being clamped together. Kary's physical attempt at a snub. But I knew that I could break down those defences, even more so because I could see the beginning of a twitch in her left eye – a sure sign that she would not be able to hold back too much longer.

"We could ask the Doctor for permission to have a dish put up. I'm sure she'd allow it, after all, it would add value to the house wouldn't it?" By now I figured that ending each stupid utterance with a question could sufficiently aggravate her into responding.

"Lots of other houses in the street have them, so there shouldn't be any problem should there?"

"Actually, they look quite trendy, what with them being black and everything don't they?"

"Of course, someone will have to ask the Doctor won't they?"

Who was the Doctor? She owned the large house we shared. We saw her regularly and she rarely refused any requests. She had a special interest in Kary – of course now I know why – and I knew that the mention of her would probably encourage Kary to respond. It was almost my last resort.

Kary's head snapped round to look at me. Defences down, or so I thought. Her eyebrows were knitted so that they formed a single unruly dark line above her small, lashless eyes. She was breathing loudly through her nose again and she had to tilt her face upwards so that she could make eye contact with me. I knew I had said enough, that any moment now, those thin purple lips would part and victory was mine. But there's a phrase I hate: Can of worms. And in my efforts to communicate, I had opened such a can as wide as I could.

Kary's arms were still at last, though dangling in the water and partly obscured by bubbles, like she had undergone some kind of hand amputation. She was wearing her blue dress, the one the Doctor had given her for her last birthday. It was made of material that looked like denim, but wasn't, and it had white stitching in the shape of flowers on the collar. Kary had loved it immediately, although I couldn't see why. It was shapeless and billowy and it tended to hang off her already rather strange shaped body, emphasising its roundness and making her look even shorter than she was. However, Kary loved it so much, she wore it only on special occasions, and it struck me as odd that she should have worn it for work. As she stood there, with splashes of water beginning to evaporate from the thin material, and visible signs of perspiration developing around the armpits, she looked like an angry little girl wearing her mother's dress.

"Clive's wife's pregnant." Through barely open lips, almost like a ventriloquist, Kary had actually spoken.

III

"Who's Clive?" Actually, I knew who Clive was, but peppering my conversation with questions seemed to be the only method of maintaining and progressing a conversation with Kary at that moment, so it was the lesser of two evils in my opinion to appear forgetful, yet still interested; less intelligent, yet willing to concede it. Looking back, I wish I had simply nodded, made her a cup of tea and gone back into the living room to sit with Angelo. Nevertheless, nothing can change matters now, and Kary reacted in exactly the way I knew she would. She snapped all the information about Clive, adding, for good measure, she had never met anyone like me who could forget every single important thing she ever told me. This was, of course, totally untrue. I remembered everything, but my motives for pretending not to remember frequently overtook the necessity of showing it.

Kary and Clive had been having an affair for six months. He was the manager of the credit control department where they both worked. He was two years older than her and, in fact, two feet taller. Both Angelo and I had spent some time sharing behind-the-hand sniggers at the thought of the two of them together.

Their physical differences were only part of the hilarity. Clive was married to Jane and they had a son, Harry, who seemed to be vile to everyone and who seemed to think that being seven years old gave him the privilege of acting like a child. Naturally, Jane was unaware of her husband's penchant for the smaller, squatter woman. She thought that Clive was doing a night school course in GCSE Biology – Angelo and I used to joke that in a way, he was. Kary took it all very seriously of course, badly applying "Kitten Cream" pink lipstick every Thursday evening at seven o'clock and then waiting with half a lager and lime at the Paphos Greek Bar round the corner from our house. Sometimes, Angelo and I used to sneak out and watch her as she waddled down the road, frequently wearing some ridiculous outfit but with an expression of total pride and excitement. Sometimes, Clive was late, and we'd survey him from our hiding place behind the big oak tree as he swung into the car park in his blue Ford Fiesta, furtively checking his hair in the mirror, and then walking gawkily like an overgrown school boy with that rising on the toes walk that some tall, thin men resort to to make themselves look less feminine. Actually, he wasn't bad looking: bright blue eyes and a ready smile, but everything about him seemed long: long face, long nose, long limbs, even his hair was longish, the remnants of a mullet lolled about the collars of his Marks & Spencers shirts. Angelo and I used to think he was like a normal sized person who had been peculiarly stretched.

The agenda for Clive and Kary's Thursdays was always the same: Clive would arrive after Kary and buy her another lager and lime and himself a lemonade with ice, no lemon. He would engage almost immediately in animated conversation with Kary who would persist in touching him – his face, his thighs, his hands. We never knew what their conversations were about because from our vantage point behind the tree, it was hard even to lip read, but we could see that both Kary and Clive were equally keen to contribute in their different ways. Although he seemed content for her to touch him, Clive was never very keen to allow Kary to kiss him in the public arena of the bar, leaning away from her when she tried. Looking back, it was astounding that Kary never realised that what she was doing was so uncomfortable for him. One evening, she tried to kiss him seventeen times; each time was like an exact replay of the last with Clive tilting his body from the waist sideways and nudging the old man sitting next to him and being stared at in wary indignation. Kary seemed content to kiss the space where Clive had been, and Clive made no comment, no facial cue of disapproval, he just, I suppose, hoped that she would get the message.

Later on, however, seemed an entirely different state of affairs. Not surprisingly, Kary's ardour appeared to be fulfilled in the privacy of the back, and front, seats of the Ford Fiesta. Always the same routine: as the car park emptied and the last few merry inmates stumbled down the concrete steps out of the pub and away, Clive and Kary would walk separately to the car and Clive would fold himself into the front seat, unlock the passenger door and Kary, frequently hopping quite literally from foot to foot, would follow.

It seems somehow indiscreet to divulge what regularly happened next, but nonetheless, pertinent to the events which followed. Angelo and I often wondered what the feel of those black plastic seats and gear stick and indication sticks felt like to poor Kary; what the steamy atmosphere which, after a few minutes prevented us from seeing much, added to the excitement for her; whether the sound of the car's aging suspension springs flexing dangerously beneath them distracted either of them or spurred them on; how, bearing physical differences in mind, the act of intercourse could actually take place. I make myself sound compassionate here. At the time of our observations, however, both Angelo and I were far from caring. We viewed Kary's Thursdays as part of our entertainment. We purchased black clothing specifically to wear on Thursday nights - to make ourselves less conspicuous. We wore footprints into the spaces between the roots of the oak tree, we made caustic comments and added running commentaries to the visual, which made us explode with laughter. We did all of this, but we never mentioned a word of it to Kary. By the time she arrived back home, we were either in our room or watching tv innocently. She would enter the house loudly, sometimes singing, and slam the door. Her cheeks were usually flushed, and either Angelo or I would say something like "Oooh Kary, your cheeks look very flushed. Is it cold out?" Kary, of course, revelled in what she saw as her "secret" and both Angelo and I thought she was thoroughly misguided when she would reply "Oh, no, actually, it's a little warm," with a knowing look on her face. Clive, of course, having ejected Kary soon after the obligatory post coital cigarette, would drive off at some speed, usually, we noticed, taking his eyes off the road even before he had reached the main road at the end of the car park, to check his watch rather feverishly. Sometimes, as part of our evening entertainment, Angelo and I would speculate as to what Clive would actually say to Jane as he returned to their suburban three bed semi, flushed and creased with Kary's passion. Would he, bruised with shame, attempt to atone his guilt by making his wife a cup of tea, sitting beside her, behaving "normally" or would he have stopped off at the petrol station on the way back and bought a bunch of wilting carnations in cellophane wrap, which she would have been delighted with (she would, in fact, tell all her friends of his generosity "..every Thursday night without fail" she might say with pride "he brings me a bunch of flowers – he's so thoughtful is Clive.") Would he sweep her off the sofa with his long thin arms – the arms which had, only fifteen minutes earlier, been encircling Kary – would he murmur those oh so familiar veiled obscenities to her as he led her to their flowery pink bedroom where, with the help of excess testosterone brought about by the fear of her discovering his infidelity, would he convince her that he loved her more than anyone? Would he invade her body with lies, and the labyrinths of her mind with deceit?

Such was our speculation.

I hated him. I actually also hated Kary. As their arrangement with each other became a regular, unchanging event, I began to lose my sense of humour, lack enthusiasm for the voyeurism which had previously been so compelling. What had started as "harmless fun" seemed now to me to be a symptom of all that was wrong in society: domination, patriarchy, lies, mistrust, greed. Somehow, by buying into the entertainment value, by laughing at them as we watched them, Angelo and I, we too were guilty of this these moral crimes because we were somehow confirming their behaviour was acceptable. Our thrill seeking was as shocking as theirs. When the realisation of this became clear to me, in great agitation, I tried to have a discussion with Angelo about the way I felt. I thought (albeit fleetingly) that we could put a stop to these meetings. I didn't care about Kary's feelings, I certainly didn't care about Clive's. Their feelings weren't the point. My feelings, the way I viewed things were the point. Angelo, I remember, looked at me blankly as I strutted and ranted in our hot living room whilst Kary was getting ready to go out. "We can't let it go on!" I remember hissing, filled with a frustration that I knew might become a real anger if I didn't at least say something. "It's morally totally wrong!" Angelo said nothing. The expression on his face didn't even register an understanding of what I was talking about. I resorted, on that occasion, to storming out of the house into the garden and making for the old swing, rusty now from age and rain, the swing we had all played on as children. Remembering that feeling of gusty abandon, I let physics and nature swing me as high as I could, just like when I was ten years old, listening to the squeaking chains, metal grinding against metal, feeling the damp early evening air rush at me from front and back, wrestling with something in my mind which gnarled my thinking and twisted my stomach. Somewhere in my imagination, we were all equal parts in a ghastly picture: Clive, Kary, Angelo and me. Four quarters of a dishonesty which I suddenly could not bear.

Keeping this from Kary – my opinion, my feelings about it all - was one of my biggest victories. Suppressing any hint or disapproval was difficult, but the lesser of two evils, since Kary's reaction to a whiff of condemnation would have been unbearable. Without the Doctor's help though, it would have been impossible. Always available to us, the Doctor came to me to sweep away those thoughts, magnified as I swung into animosity that damp, warm, late Summer evening. She was wise. She listened. She didn't judge and she always gave sound advice. She explained to me that decisions were human and that humans made mistakes. She asked me to consider the way in which people pursue happiness in different ways. She challenged me to stop wasting energy on hating anyone when I should, in fact, be pursuing my own happiness. She urged me to back away from that sensation of frustration. She spoke about ethics. Morals. The fluidity of them both. She seemed right. Basically, she made me wonder why someone else's personal arrangements should matter to me. She made me question why I should take things so seriously.

So back in our kitchen Kary's soliloquy droned on, shaking me from my thoughts and reasoning: "… and he told me that they slept separately. I said to him it must have been an immaculate conception or something. I mean, how can a woman get pregnant without, you know…" Still ferociously scrubbing something in the now murky washing up water. "I can't believe it, I really can't. I mean," she sounded exasperated now and her hands settled into stillness as she turned her head slowly to me, "I mean, why aren't I pregnant?" I could see that she was crying and tears left sad, crooked white lines in her too-brown face make-up, mascara smudges were visible along the bottom of her eyes. I couldn't help feeling sorry for her, only for a second but long enough to convince her that she could rely on my sympathy. "Oh poor Kary." I gathered her in my arms and felt her pathetic sobs against my shoulder.

And there we were: me skimming Kary's back from shoulder blade to coccyx, feeling the static electricity from her polyester dress begin to ignite, feeling the dampness from her pruned hands on the small of my own back, feeling the throb of new bruising on my forehead from the bathroom door, hearing Angelo chuckling at something on tv and smelling a mix of detergent and perspiration which could have been a mix of us all.

IV

As children, we had all grown up in this house. Simultaneously happy and confused, we got through our early years together not attending school, which we thought was normal. We were educated at home. The Doctor provided us with an individualised curriculum which meant that Angelo excelled at sport, Kary at maths and my speciality was literature. My room was awash with books for as long as I can remember and I loved it. By the time I was ten years old I had read all of Austen, Dickens, Lawrence and Shakespeare, was familiar with the raunchy Restoration poets and I loved Aldous Huxley. The Doctor saw to it that we were regularly monitored in every respect. This meant not only a health check, but also academic testing on a six weekly basis in our specialised subject until we were eighteen. After that we were thrust out into a world that we had otherwise experienced vicariously via the Doctor, books and videos and of course, our annual seaside holidays in Devon.

Looking at it now, with the knowledge that I have, outsiders viewed us with some considerable interest. Putting aside everything else, our upbringing alone made us "different". The house in which we lived – still do live

– provided warmth and safety; large and Victorian with a huge oak door painted green and a noisy antique lion's head door-knocker (which was rarely knocked). Even now, I still think of the high ceilings as unusually high – as I child, I felt like I was looking up into the heavens at that orange and cream painted woodchip, and in a way, I was. The hall of our house was – is - spectacular: long and thin with colourful Minton tiles, octagonal shaped terracotta and squares of blue, rectangles and pentagons of pale orange and triangles of white following a repeated pattern from the oak door to the kitchen. Some of the tiles are broken or cracked, mended in an unconvincing way, replaced by something similar in places, if you looked very closely. Lines of aged dirt and Victorian grime remain between each tile. It wasn't important, it isn't important now. Kary spent time as a child counting the shapes and working out a mathematical formula for the pattern. She found it fascinating that someone so long ago had devised a series of shapes which fitted together so well, and kept fitting together, despite the dirt and the weight of footprints and the attempts to clean. From my own point of view, the idea of such beautiful colours brightening this peculiar area in our house, never being covered, never changing, was a source of immense interest. The hall leads to everywhere in the house. You cannot avoid it, and this fact alone gave it a kind of superiority and thrust its splendour and necessity on each of us. Once when I was about eight years old one of the white tiles which had been loose for a while and which jangled each time anyone walked on it became too much of a temptation for me and, using the butter knife from the kitchen, I eased it out of its place in one of the patterns. The tile was about two centimetres deep, and this surprised me as I inspected it closely. It was the smallest shape in the pattern: a triangle of white with each side measuring about three centimetres. It left a black soily hole in the floor next to the larger blue tile. I can remember feeling suddenly upset that the arrangement had been spoiled and that even the removal of the smallest piece could destroy the blueprint we all knew so well. Quickly I fitted it back into its place, pressing it down with my full weight on the palms of both hands, like a nurse giving cardiac massage to a dying patient, feeling the grinding residue beneath the tile, painfully ashamed that I had given in to curiosity, that I had allowed myself to dare to change or investigate, that I had begun to question what was a material fact. Each time I hear that grating loose tile in our hallway, I am reminded of this latent shame.

No-one ever knew of course, and Kary did devise a formula for the pattern, explaining it with great authority and glee to an audience of me and Angelo. Neither of us really listened or cared, but we were incredulous as to why she would want to know how the pattern was put together.

It's only now that I understand why she felt so driven to work it out.

V

_____

After Kary's discovery that Clive was to be a father again, she underwent a change. I think she made a few visits to the Doctor, but of course, that was entirely confidential and anyway, I'm not certain that the Doctor could have helped her much. Kary was such a focused person that we were not surprised when she seemed to become very quickly obsessed with getting pregnant. Tabloid psychology quite rightly suggests that people want most what they are least likely to get. The fact that Kary's lover had produced one child with another woman, even though it was his wife, was bad enough as far as Kary was concerned. The unfaithfulness was on its head though and for Clive to have been unfaithful to Kary was ironically enough to make her keener. She was always highly competitive but now saw the whole arrangement between her and Clive as a real challenge, with the aim of having Clive get her pregnant as soon as possible. Up to that point, Kary's interest in children had been limited to walking past them on the way to work each morning. She had been particularly cool towards the concept of childbirth, enjoying instead the safety of protected sex with Clive and grazing on paracetamol for a couple of days each month, never mentioning any disappointment or brooding over magazine articles about babies or showing any desire to coo coo over real life babies in buggies in shops. In fact, she frequently heaved a visible sigh of relief when her period came, muttering things like "Thank God for that" and reducing Angelo to a blushing heap as she left open packets of tampons in the downstairs toilet. In short, the sudden realisation of Clive's fertility jolted her biological clock into action.

At first, cynics though we are, we thought her prime motive was to secure a permanent relationship with Clive – it is, after all, a trap that many women (and men) fall into in an effort to "settle down", to "ensnare" effectively. The production of children, the meeting of two sets of genes, the successful collision, traditionally requires affection at the very least between the two parties, and frequently either follows or elicits the notion of love. Or at least that's how it seems to me. Therefore we thought that Kary either felt, or wanted to feel or wanted Clive to feel something she could call "love". We thought it was Clive that she wanted, and that a more permanent understanding was what she was angling for. We thought a baby would be the catalyst to this fantasy, but would probably be superfluous – maybe less even than that – if Kary's plan went awry and Clive would not play ball. We may have been right at the beginning. She may have really wanted Clive, but something happened to change her priorities, to make her think again. Put very simply, Kary could not seem to conceive. Give her her due, she tried everything with Clive: she demanded to see him more often – we don't know to this day how he managed to appease his conscience on this one, what with Jane being pregnant, but their Thursdays became their Tuesdays and Thursdays;

she tampered with the condoms using the needles from the needlework box, pricking minute holes through their wrappers, she even brought him home so as, she said, to ensure more space for comfortable and "conception-likely" positions. Kary's plan was, of course, a secret from Clive who just must have thought his luck was in. One Tuesday night at our house and in desperation, Kary laced his lemonade with vodka. I think her plan was to loosen him up sufficiently so that ideas about contraception failed to be part of his plan. I'm not sure she was victorious but I do know poor Clive was unconscious until 7 am the next morning, leaving in a hurry and they didn't see each other for a couple of weeks after that. During this time, Kary hatched another plot, she would tell him she was on the pill – naturally, she wasn't. For two months, Angelo and I observed Kary's ever more active love life. We also coped with her disappointment on the 15th of each month which materialised as foul moods, profanities and floods of tears, often simultaneously. She was inconsolable so we didn't try to comfort her, we kept out of her way. It would have been hopeless to have suggested anything about giving it time or conceptual ideas about fate or God stepping in, preventing her pregnancy from happening because it was intrinsically "wrong" because Kary would have gone berserk.

Naturally, I had my own ideas which could certainly not be voiced to Kary. I was pleased that she was unsuccessful in her attempts to get pregnant. I failed to see why she would want Clive's child, or why she thought she had the right to be party to the deceit that would undoubtedly destroy his wife. Or how she thought she would be able to look after a baby. I was not mad with anger, but I did tackle my issues with the Doctor, who listened quietly and then suggested that my feelings showed a finely honed moral idealism which was commendable but not advisable "in this day and age". She questioned me on my thoughts about science and religion. This stopped me in my tracks, and I'm sure this was the desired outcome. We had been taught science but we had not been brought up in a religious household, had never attended church, but as children had simply been schooled in religious education so we knew the names of some belief systems but were neither encouraged nor discouraged to become involved in any. Consequently, the doctor's question made me analyse what propelled me into such irritation and why I could not – would not – simply tell Kary what my feelings were. After all, real friends can share opinions. But then the Doctor reminded me that we were all more than "real friends" and this necessarily makes revealing strong feelings to each other more difficult.

Nevertheless, the Doctor's question made me think. An all-powerful God, by its very nature, cannot be a democratic one can it? Maybe, I thought, if a God was involved in the decision making process which prevented Kary from conceiving, then the decision transcended mere science, and was based in what was actually right in the opinion of that God. Science, though, could provide some logical answers, some reasons: x didn't react with y, so there can be no z. However, surely science itself must be considered as an undemocratic God then since it is solely responsible for the reaction in the first place.

Anyway, Kary's failure in the baby department gave rise to a clarity about her motives, and we soon became absolutely aware of her desire not to simply trap Clive or win him, in a bizarre competition, away from his wife. It was, we realised, the baby that Kary wanted.

Some time into the fourth babyless month, I arrived home to find Kary's winter coat hung up in the hall. This was unusual because she was generally the last one home and at first I suspected she was ill and had left work early.

"Kary!" I called from the hallway, taking off my shoes, "You ok?"

There was no instant reply, and for a moment I had a horrible feeling I was going to find Kary and Clive taking advantage of an afternoon's ovulation (Kary had taken to testing herself and had filled the bathroom cabinet with a year's supply of "the most reliable ovulation test on the market today"). I stood for a while in the hallway with this image forming in my mind, trying to think of ways to prevent the thought from fully developing, when I heard the rustle of paper. Relieved that something had happened to distract my thinking, I rallied and made for the living room where Kary sat alone, reading a magazine.

"Oh hi," I said breezily, a little relieved and flounced noisily down on the sofa opposite her. Kary continued reading as if I wasn't there. Her red pinprick eyes had been crying again but they were reading with such vigour that her eyeballs visibly traced out each letter, each word on the page in a twitchy, irregular movement. Magazine reading had never been one of Kary's hobbies, but it didn't surprise me that she had taken to this pastime, especially given that one of the puffs on the front page proclaimed "Foetal abduction: it happened to me."

Kary continued reading as if I wasn't there. After a while, I left her to it and went to my room to think.

VI

It was the following day when I was eating breakfast that Kary and I had our next conversation. Every Saturday morning was the same, Angelo had a lie-in and Kary usually went shopping. I liked to get up early and just sit alone in our kitchen. I liked to watch the garden change with the seasons and I liked the peace and quiet of the morning. I could feel a comfortable solitude, and the hum of the central heating coupled with the smell of tea and toast made me relax into my well-worn wooden kitchen chair, thinking nothing in particular. So Kary's arrival into the kitchen was both unexpected and unwelcome. She had rattled down the hallway, muttering loudly to herself. The kitchen door was always wedged open but she kicked at it irritatedly as she entered. I felt annoyed that she had disturbed my Saturday morning ritual and didn't feel inclined to greet her in any way so continued sipping my tea and watching the last of the leaves on the apple tree cling onto life. Kary was therefore the first to speak.

"Do you know what 'foetal abduction' is?"

"Yes." I replied without looking at her, "Some woman in America had her baby snatched out of her pregnant body."

It was the simplest I could put it. I had read the article in Kary's magazine. Written in the usual sensational style, it was a most peculiar true story of a pregnant woman who had indeed had her unborn baby removed and kidnapped from her body by a so-called "friend" who desperately wanted a child. The woman miraculously survived despite massive blood loss, but the article went into some gory detail as to the surgical procedure that was required to perform such an amateur operation, as well as the way in which the "friend" had feigned her own pregnancy by gaining lots of weight, even convincing her husband and family that she was actually expecting. Naturally, she had been arrested and the happy-ever-after story told how the child, a girl had grown up perfectly normally.

"Mmm." said Kary, "What do you think?"

Totally thrown by this – Kary never asked for anyone's opinion and I suddenly felt most uncomfortable, both regarding the subject matter and the request – I stumbled momentarily for words. Impatient as ever, Kary snapped nastily at me, "Well?" And I said the first thing that came into my head.

"I think she was mad."

We stared in contemplative silence as if we had simultaneously and suddenly noticed something in our communal blackspot.

After a while, Kary said, "What did she use?"

I looked at her and said "A scalpel."

Kary swung her face round to mine, and with furrowed brows said, " No stupid. What did she *use* to get the *information*." Not a question now – a demand really.

Feeling about five years old again, I told her it was thought that the woman found information on performing Caesarian sections on the internet.

"It was *thought*?"

I was thrown again now. It's funny how your psychology works. Suddenly lacking in any confidence in the information I had given sparked off by Kary's incredulity, vocabulary took refuge and I could only nod in an effort to add anything to the exchange we were having.

And there we both were in a freeze frame: Kary leaning forward, head tilted up towards me, her eyes burning into mine. And me: Doubtful and eager to please. Becoming ever more aware of the tears of perspiration running down my back and the developing twitch in my left eyelid. Without looking away, Kary spoke first:

"Well whoever invented the internet's got a lot to answer for," she said quietly.

We didn't know it, but Angelo had caught the last part of our exchange and he entered the kitchen yawning loudly and mindlessly rearranging his somehow beautifully scruffy hair.

"What's all this about the internet? Are we getting it?" he asked lazily.

"No." Kary switched her attention to him now. "What do you think about foetal abduction?"

"Feet and what?" asked Angelo, noisily filling the kettle and yawning disinterestedly again.

I really hoped Kary would leave it at that. Angelo would have absolutely no clue what she was talking about and she would only become agitated if she had to explain.

"Oh Angelo." I laughed and rose, skipping over to the sink where he was already making himself tea and snaked my arms round his waist, kissing the pretty nape of his neck lightly, "What are you going to do today?" He turned to face me with his usual smile.

Sometimes these distraction tactics worked because Kary could be sufficiently disconcerted by the sudden change of subject that she would give up ideas about questioning. Today, however, no such luck; she stamped to her feet, visibly shaking, jolting the kitchen table so that my mug of tea rocked dangerously for a second.

"Oh, come on, you heard." Her voice was shrill and we knew that this meant she would not let the matter rest. "Foetal abduction is when a child is stolen from the mother's womb." A most uncomfortable pause. "What do you think about it for God's sake?"

Poor Angelo had absolutely no idea how to react and I felt him tighten under the strain of Kary's persistence. She might as well have asked him a question on nuclear physics, and I felt a surge of protectiveness flood my thinking. Before I realised it the words had left my lips.

"Don't ask Angelo, Kary. You know he probably doesn't know anything about it." As soon as it was said, I regretted it, and Kary bridled immediately. To soften it, I added "It's a girl thing, pregnancy. Angelo doesn't know much about babies. Maybe we should let him read your magazine later."

But it was too late. Kary saw my response as confrontational and unnecessary and her first port of call in such situations was attack. She strutted over to us, standing as close as she could to Angelo, knowing that his weakness would allow her to get away with any insult. Her almost invisible neck bent oddly backwards so that her face was close up to his, her eyes blazing with animosity, she spat the words out to him: "You are so stupid Angelo. Stupid and hopeless. You *should* know about these things. Only an imbecile would admit to not knowing." Her lisp was at its worse when she was most angry, and the sibilance of her outburst resulted in sticky saliva spraying out of her mouth and landing on both Angelo and me in a physical confirmation of the depth of her disapproval of us. Even though her outbursts were no surprise to us, each time she vented her abusive frustrations out on us was equally painful, equally raw and equally destructive. In an ironic way, each time chipped away at our confidence, our happiness and our sense of normality, but each time hardened something in me – maybe it was my heart or my "self", but it gave me an illusion of a growing inner strength. Each time I survived another onslaught, the twanging pain was always followed by a deep resentment, an internal litany of abuse in response, a cognitive playscript in which the typically British audience took my side – the side of the underdog – and booed Kary, who was later thrown into the ashes from which I rise. For Angelo though, it was different, and as this thought festered in my brain, Kary continued, this time prodding Angelo's chest with her stubby finger.

"You're a fool Angelo, a complete fool."

A pause. Would it stop there? Experience told us that if we stood perfectly still and averted our eyes in these situations, sometimes Kary would stop. But not always. Today, she advanced on Angelo, shoving him hard in the shoulder with the fist of her right hand. Angelo stumbled backwards, and as I reached out to stop him from falling over completely, Kary slapped my face with the back of her hand, sending me reeling sideways away from Angelo and tripping like a drunk onto the cold kitchen floor tiles.

"Stop trying to help him!" She yelled down at me as the sting of the slap was overtaken by the pain from hitting my head on the hard floor, "You're always doing that! You're not his mother you know."

From my vantage point at floor level, I watched as she turned on her heels and scurried out of the kitchen. Only when we heard the front door slam did Angelo come to my aid, kissing my injured face, my head and my tears and whispering placations and endearments with hot breath against my neck.

VII

_____

The weather was bleak and grey, the pavements wet and greasy. Slimy puddles had collected forming irregular patterns near the curb offering temporary wobbly reflections of benign passers-by.

I could feel damp seeping through my clothes making the pores of my skin prick with cold. I was conscious of my own breathing and inexplicably began timing inhalations and exhalations against my footsteps, head down, shivering. I didn't need to look up. I knew it so well.

When Kary had not returned home after three hours of waiting, Angelo and I had decided that we should look for her. I knew town was a magnet for her. There was something about the place that she found utterly compulsive. I had tried to enjoy it with her a couple if times and I tried to put myself in her shoes now, think where she would go, what she would do.

When the cold air caught at the back of my throat together with a mix of familiar flavours, I knew I was almost there. I didn't want to look up yet. Instinctively I knew that the peppery taste of the town was about to be replaced by a hint of smoky savouriness that she couldn't resist relishing, and my heart beat and my breathing and my footsteps automatically quickened. And it's only when I rounded the corner into Market Street that I gave myself a visual treat, loving the clumsy asymmetry, as she would have, of the stalls with their stripy canopies and flapping plastic sheets. I slowed down and stopped for a moment, allowing my eyes to accommodate to the view: A portal into a better time; a splash of colour; a touched up snapshot by an amateur photographer entitled "Saturday".

I strolled into the picture. A hive of controlled activity, of woollen hats, fingerless gloves. The scene seemed practiced somehow, unnatural. I felt like a comfortable extra and found myself listening in to different conversations as I passed through. Overlapping, interrupting, a mixture of sounds, voices, questions, statements, demands. It was warmer there, protected as I was between stalls, brushing past others, browsing aimlessly, unable to stop in the wake of those walking ahead of me, anyway not wanting to spoil the picture.

My eyes glanced over the Aladdin's cave of cheap necessities – batteries next to home baked bread, boiled sweets next to Band Aids. Stallholders varied their sales pitch from serene endurance of the heavy atmosphere to loud cat calls imitating the call and response of the Black American churches. A woman wearing a body warmer and long acrylic finger nails fumbled for some change unsuccessfully clutching at the pennies like an inept toddler. To me, it was a scene from a comedy programme. To Kary, it was heaven.

The underwear stall was festooned with purple, red and black g-strings I knew of as the sort that Kary had begun buying. A silky basque flapped in the breeze, plastic suspender hooks clinked against the stall's metal poles like an obscene tap dance. There was a young man placing a pack of forty denier "American Tan" tights into a floral bag for an elderly woman. He was smiling downwards, and I wondered exactly what crossed his mind as he sold the crotchless panties and fishnet stockings. I wondered whether he had seen Kary today.

I gulped back a breath of someone else's gritty exhaled cigarette smoke and momentarily experience a vicarious, second hand nicotine induced high, but then a waft of salty heat from the hot pie stall took me by surprise, and I knew that the shot of meaty steam would linger on my clothes like a ghost until long after I got home.

A tinny mixture of musical sound, vaguely familiar as a favourite childhood song jangled amidst the atmosphere and then faded out back into the past. The past we spent together: me, Angelo and Kary, and although I continued walking, I expected a song from the same era to fade in at any moment. I was jolted then back into the present, back into the reason for my being there. Looking for Kary. And my warm affable mood became infiltrated by a musky dankness, sweeping me away from the picture, out once again into real life. Cold again. Resisting the temptation to look back. Resisting the temptation to work anything out. Sometimes it's best to let things lie. This had not been the first time Kary had lost her temper, and it certainly wouldn't be the last.

VIII

Angelo was also looking for Kary. He knew all the likely places because she spoke to him more than she spoke to me, always had done. Despite the fact that we had always been together, Kary had always vied for his attention and attempted to push me out of the way.

Memories of my childhood, though, are happy ones, I think I can remember sitting in my buggy, which I shared with Kary and Angelo. There was a soft blanket being shared across our little laps and I seem to remember sitting in the middle – always in the middle. Kary, crying, shook a pink plastic rattle madly, gradually becoming more and more frantic as, I guess, it became clear to her she was being ignored. Her little face screwed up like a cartoon caricature and angry tears rolled down her cheeks, leaving little transparent silvery lines and resting like a puddle in the crease in her chin. Suddenly, I remember a sharp jabbing pain on my forehead. Kary was smashing her rattle repeatedly against my face. Later on I have a distinct memory of being wedged in the same buggy between Kary and Angelo, both of them staring benignly out, their pale blue eyes transfixed on a spot somewhere in the future, and me, pawing their shoulders with my toddler's hand, desperate for their attention, but invariably failing to get it, desperate to drag them back to the present, already desperate to be like them. Of course, I didn't know that then. What I did know, even from that age, was that Angelo was beautiful. The most beautiful face ever. Ringlets of golden hair framed what was to become, to me, an almost perfect face. Even as a child, it was clear what the future held, and his pink lips were only ever going to be responsible for creating the cravings of weak-kneed females.

Psychologists would have us believe that no feeling is permanent, and that we simply cannot maintain these feelings for ever. But for as long as I could remember I had loved Angelo and I loved him with a permanence beyond psychology. By the time I was fifteen, I was so deeply in love with him that I would have done anything for him. Anything at all.

It was Angelo who found Kary. She was sitting in a café in town, sipping a cappuccino. He told me he just approached her, sat down, and she apologised. He said they sat there for a while and then they walked the long way home in virtual silence. I had been home for a while by that time. I felt agitated when they arrived. My day had been ruined and my routine had been spoilt, but the sight of Angelo's beaming face was a real cheer-up. Kary couldn't meet my eye and I felt pleased that this was a sign of contrition. Somewhere in that misshapen head of hers there must have been an area set aside for regret. I wondered what psychologists might make of her.

That night, Angelo stroked my hair as we lay in the dark and I listened to his breathing even out and deepen and his heartbeat steady until he had drifted into a peaceful sleep. My room was warm and musty and we were both a little tacky with perspiration; parts of our bodies were stuck together: part of my belly on his hip, my thigh on his, the soft fleshy under part of my arm resting on his chest. The duvet was pulled up to my chin and up to Angelo's shoulders and I felt more comfortable than I had ever felt. Our house was absolutely silent. The central heating had been off long enough for the house to have stopped clicking and creaking back into shape, the water was undisturbed in the pipes, even the nocturnal creatures outside seemed to be elsewhere. There was no sound from Kary's attic bedroom. She had retired to bed early, and alone – after all it was Saturday so no Clive. We had not heard a single sound from her room after that, neither had any of us spoken about the incident. Such was the pattern of our lives.

The thoughts of the day diluted and I must have fallen into a deep, contented sleep, awoken early next morning by the sound of Angelo getting dressed and feeling as if it had only been a moment ago that Angelo's flesh and mine had been so beautifully connected.

"Ah," I whispered, stretching my arms out of the warmth of the duvet, "the sound of denim against firm flesh – I love it."

Angelo grinned at me with luminous white teeth through the semi darkness.

"What time is it?" I asked, sitting up and trying to focus on the alarm clock.

"Only 7.30. It's my turn to work today," Angelo was slipping on his tee shirt now and I could clearly see the logo on the top right corner, a yellow key with a smiling face giving a cartoon wave. Angelo had worked in the shop in town forever – "key cutting and cobbling" as Kary used to say. He had started there at the age of eighteen and never complained or grumbled. He just went to work. I always secretly admired his tenacity and skill. He worked with an old, old man who had opened the shop before any of us were born and who had taken on the smell of warm rubber and the squint and stoop of someone who perpetually concentrates very hard. Already Angelo must have mended thousands of pairs of shoes and cut millions of keys. For this alone I admired him immensely.

I felt the disappointment niggle. I'd forgotten it was Angelo's Sunday to work and instantly regressed to adolescence.

"Ring in sick," I whinged, "I'll do it for you. Pass me your mobile. I'll tell him you've got a stomach upset or a migraine or something." I held out my arms like a zombie, wiggling my fingers, knowing that the last thing that Angelo would do would be to let anyone down, knowing instead that he would leap across the bed and embrace me.

"Behave yourself," he breathed into my ear, hugging me tightly, "I'll be back by 3."

I let him go, maintaining the facial expression of a reluctant teenager until long after he had left the room and wondering why I felt so thoroughly put out today. Lying back after Angelo had gone, I thought about Kary's outburst and wondered what the day would hold in store. I knew that if I didn't get out of bed and do something, I would begin to feel wretched. Already my skin was beginning to take on that familiar prickly feel, almost like my body was preparing, hardening up, getting ready.

With still no sound from Kary's room, I decided to take a shower and go out before she got up.

The house felt grimy and the bathroom hadn't been cleaned for a while. A thin towel was strewn like a dead animal on the floor, limp and damp, around it a corona outline of stale bath water. Evidence of dust caught along the white glossed skirting boards made the room feel sour, scummy. Paint on the walls was discoloured with damp and finger and body marks, darkened and dirtied. The perspex shower doors were opaque with dried droplets of water yet sticky to the touch and the stippled shower tray was slippery with rejected shampoo and disused soap, and clumps of dull, tangled hair were caught lifelessly across the plughole. When I looked, I saw that the water in the toilet bowl was sufficiently brown and still as to make the whole room feel dirty and unhygienic and as I approached it, a smell akin to halitosis seemed to be emitting from the toilet itself, contributing to the general aroma of warm urine and stale bleach. Someone's dark pubic hairs were stuck hopelessly to the inside rim of the toilet seat, poking strangely diagonally outwards like hairline cracks on the white porcelain. Limescale formed pervasively along the inside lip so that there was a feeling of general abandon, of haplessness or priorities more important than mere cleanliness. Sharp slanted sunlight periodically cut across the room like a searchlight illuminating cobwebs, heavy with droplets of moisture and grey dust hanging tiredly onto the knobbly dried rivulets of off-white gloss paint in the corners of the ceiling. Every now and then their intricate patterns changed according to some otherwise unfelt draught.

Spots of black mould on the shower curtain seemed alive with microbes or bacteria or something unnerving or potentially fatal, and my urge to stay clean was compromised by the unfairness of having to do so in such unclean surroundings. A box of tampons had been opened and the contents had fallen, or had been left, in the wash basin where they lay, like one of those pictures of viruses seen from a microscope. Blue-grey gloop festered around the base of the taps, and spat up toothpaste remained welded into white porous pustules inside the basin, above which was a rectangular mirror, old, unframed and silver brown around the edge. My reflected face concealed none of my growing contempt, although the expression could have been mistaken for alarm. I noticed how sharp my features were becoming and how frequent frowning was developing two identical vertical lines of about 1cm in length between my eyebrows and how, even when my expression was intentionally lightened, their ghost remained. Like most people, the distraction of a mirror invoked closed examination of its subject. Coming face to face with one's self – or at least one's reflected face – seems always compulsive. My eyes were early morning bloodshot. My skin, milky white and comparatively flawless with youth – even on close inspection by turning my face into various contorted shapes, I could find no really serious blemishes - had always been something I had been proud of. My hair needed to be washed, it was greasy and two shades darker than it should have been, not exactly "lank" (I liked the popular magazine lingo) but as I pushed my hand through it, it lay rather heavily between my fingers, leaving a miniscule residue of glistening sebum which I examined closely on my finger tips. My lips: I loved my lips: bulging full and liver-red; I leaned forward, very close to the mirror and licked my lips producing a shimmering sheen of saliva, reminding myself that unusually, and rather attractively, the upper lip was slightly fuller than the bottom one which made me look interesting, pre-raphaelite and conventionally seductive. Men had often commented on my lips, suggesting quite blatantly what was on their mind: "Come and suck on this darlin'" or "Why don't you let me introduce you to something tasty". Others held animated conversations about unrelated subjects whilst not taking their eyes off my lips. If I wore lipstick of course, it was worse (or better depending on your viewpoint) and complete strangers in the street (usually male though sometimes not) would actually do a double take. I liked the attention my lips provoked. My teeth, which should have been uneven, had been straightened, remodelled, "sorted out" by painful orthodentistry in my early teens. They were sticky with morning plaque. I was tempted not to brush them, maybe not for days, to tease the decay into beginning and then to assault it with dental products. The idea made me smile – to play Russian Roulette with years of compliant but successful dental torture would launch me into the realms of sado-masochism, wouldn't it? Just imagining the dentist's face – so ingratiatingly self-congratulatory at having transformed my entire dental profile, his great Dracula-like face beaming into mine – and how disapproving and disappointed he would be, was enough to cheer me up; even the thought of that tingling sensation, not quite pain, brought about by the onset of decay seemed oddly attractive.

Sometimes, very little about my face was satisfactory to me, and the thought of ruining something about myself, about my appearance, seemed to present me with the ultimate power. For a moment I considered whether I was getting into self-harm. I quickly dismissed this as creative thinking and grabbed my toothbrush as confirmation that the thought would never be complete in the act. My gums responded to the toothpaste by giving off a fizzling, fiery sensation which I enjoyed so much, I inhaled some of the cooled bathroom air briskly to enhance the feeling, loving the shock of mintiness spreading swiftly down into my lungs and then grinding my teeth together, wincing slightly at the dry, crunching particles of toothpaste between my perfect teeth obtusely putting me in mind of high quality mint chocolate, only stopping to respond to Kary's insistent knocking at the door and her muffled shouts which sounded, through my reverie, like she was saying "Hurry up, bitch."

IX

We all thought Clive's life must have been really weird. There he was, father of a mad child, husband of a pregnant woman and, how could we describe it: gigolo? Lover? Sperm donor more like, to Kary. The number of times he was summoned to see her had increased to three in a week, and, we suspected, now included regular lunch time assignations. We would hear them: him groaning and her moaning encouragement to him, the rhythmic thumping becoming part of our routine. Despite this though, Kary did not conceive and she carried around with her a kind of blueness, a sadness mingled with a tangible anger and a hair trigger contempt for everyone and everything around her, including Clive. She took to ridiculing him, considering us to be the awaiting audience. Clive's resolve was visibly ebbing away. Once in particular, Clive appeared in our kitchen. He looked shattered. His face was wrinkled and greyish with exhaustion and his hair seemed damp-thin, scraped back. Sitting at the pine table, slumped really, his shirt unbuttoned revealing a scrawny but surprisingly virile hairy chest, he breathed noisily. He looked depressed, bereft, tired of it all. His eyelids were swollen and heavy and he rested his stubbly chin forlornly on his cupped hand, an elbow placed dangerously near the edge of the table. At any moment, I expected his arm to slip abruptly off the edge, jolting him rudely into normality. Because of this, not wanting to alarm him, I coughed a gentle cough as I entered the kitchen, feigning pleasant surprise on seeing him.

"Oh, Clive," I said lightly, "How lovely to see you."

Clive raised a pathetic, uncomfortable smile and sat up straight, clearing his throat nervously.

"Would you like a cuppa?" I looked past him and walked to the kettle. I sounded breezy, and I liked the way I had used the informal "cuppa". It wasn't a word I usually used but it was intended to make him feel more at ease because despite myself I was actually beginning to feel sorry for him. Granted, I wasn't happy with his and Kary's arrangement but I also knew what she was capable of and, with a skewed logic, believed that he didn't need any more spite or disapproval, least of all from me, not outwardly anyway. From the kitchen sink, I could see the back of his gaunt body. A bald spot was radiating from the crown of his head and above his hunched-again narrow shoulders was a neck, creased and a little spotty – that yellow headed kind – in amongst potholey scar tissue from previously spotty times. His lack of response I took as a sign of discomfort and immediately experienced a bizarre feeling of superiority, finding myself taking on the classic pose of dominance mixed with defence: chin up, jaw relaxed, arms folded, legs idly crossed at the ankle whilst leaning casually back against the kitchen unit. Ridiculous of course, since Clive could not see me - I was standing behind him.

Noise from the kettle provided the only sound effect in the room and I considered for a moment whether to interrupt its rattly homeliness when Clive, without turning to face me, mumbled "You must think I'm a complete fool."

Immediately, the balance of power changed; that self-effacing manner, that self-deprecation took away any possibility for me to get one over on him, even if I wanted to. It interested me that I could tell he had all areas covered.

"What do you mean?" The ball back in his court now, with me still standing behind him.

The kettle had clicked and the silence that followed added to the dramatic tension.

It took a while for Clive to speak but when he did it was with surprising vocal clarity. Turning in his chair so that his long thighs swirled round from under the table, and looking directly at me he said calmly "I can't keep up with her."

It would have been laughable if it hadn't have been so true.

I said nothing, it seemed for the best.

Clive fed off the silence, losing his calm and becoming animated and agitated at once, throwing his head into his hands, rocking back and forth.

"I am such a complete, utter fool. I let her rule my life. I don't know why." Tailing off at the end, unable to connect his thoughts. I tried to place his accent. Not local, definitely not from round here, the intonation was all wrong; confusing in its unpredictability. His difference, his situation, his predicament, all made me feel sorry for him and I wrestled with the possibility that I should embrace him, like a mother holds a needy child. It could pass for propriety, I thought, given that he was trusting me with such personal information. I could imagine having his bristly sharp chin nestling into my shoulder, my hand stroking the back of his head and spotty neck, feeling his spindly arms pull me closer.

I decided against it and instead went with nodding in benign agreement. Suspended in the moment, we endured that silence again. Silence: such a powerful tool in communication.

"I can't carry on. I don't even like her." There was that intonation again: alien and imploring. He needed an answer from me.

"Well now," I began, moving to sit opposite him and taking on the manner of one of those car mechanics who is about to break the news that your car has failed its MOT, was about to list a series of serious, possibly fatal faults that you probably couldn't afford to fix and should certainly not have been depending on to safely get you from A to B. For effect, I actually did take a sharp intake of breath which whistled through the even gaps in my teeth. "Kary is a very complex person Clive." Using his name to end the sentence: another superiority tactic. "She can be exceedingly focused and when she wants something, that's all that matters." I leaned forward, my hands clasped in determined truth, but not touching him, "We know how she works, but it's no easier for us. You have to let her get it out of her system."

"But I can't." Clive regressed to adolescence, whingy and miserable, withdrawing his interest immediately, overstressing the word "can't", slumping further into his seat, averting his gaze. In an equal and opposite reaction,

I leaned further forward across the table, extending my arms but still not touching him, not the car mechanic now, but the not-so-nasty childless step mother, having seen a chink in the errant step son's armour, keen to forge some sort of relationship. "Clive, look at me." He looked at me. "Take some advice from me." (I was actually quite good at this) "If you can't live with it, tell her it's over. Be totally straight with her. It's the only way, believe me. She'll be absolutely fine and you can go back to Jane, forget what happened and enjoy your life." Now I was on a campaign, like an Evangelist; on a mission. "Break free from her now Clive, you can't go on like this can you? Of course she'll be pretty pissed off at first, but you know we'll look after her, and really, you should be with your wife and family." There it was: the ace card, played: the wife and family jab. I sat back, aware that throughout my short speech, Clive's eyes had scanned my face and had rested on my lips, watching them animate and authorise. I realised that Clive's weakness lay in his hormones, and that, even with his apparent depression, he still couldn't suppress that maleness which, after all, was the root of his problem with Kary. A mild irritation made me frown and this seemed to kick start him into responding.

"OK," he said, "I'll tell her."

I smiled.

He was right though, I thought he was a complete, utter fool.

X

We were fifteen years old and on our annual holiday in Devon. The weather, as it always seemed to be, was glorious; cloudless blue skies hung like a dream above the placid turquoise sea. It was August. We lived in shorts and tee shirts. Everyone was happy. My face ached with smiling and squinting against the summer sunlight.

We were staying in one of those whitewashed, holiday-let cottages typically only a short stroll from the beach. Ivy grew big and freely around the front door and upstairs windows, and wild jasmine crept sneakily up the centre of the house, its scent heavy and saccharine-sweet, extending out into the overgrown garden. Inside the house it was cramped in a cosy, Devonian kind of way, and cool. The outdated kitchen contained a few utensils, plates and dishes thrown together from various different sets and an archaic shiny electric kettle which took an age to boil. An enormous piece of well-used pine, scarred with age lines and knotty memories, acted as a chopping board and work surface. There were two home made cupboards painted blue, remnants from the 1950s, hung precariously on the wall. There was a deep, white Belfast sink and a single discoloured silver tap – cold of course – which dripped rhythmically leaving a permanent grey residue in the shape of a heart where it dropped. Beneath the sink was a curtain of madly coloured material, puckered at the top and attached to a white nylon string strung tightly between the edge of the sink and a brass hook on the wall, behind which various largely untouched cleaning chemicals and sponges lurked bacterially on bowed, stained, thin wooden shelves. There was a constant smell of damp, despite the warmth – not unpleasant - and the cheap, ill-fitting floor covering squelched humorously in certain spots. The gas cooker wouldn't light without great argument, resulting in a frequent clacky aroma of methane and match sulphur. We didn't bother to clean the windows, and we doubted anyone else did (including the landlord) so, in place of curtains or a blind, a thick sticky layer filtered out the sunlight and picture postcard view of the moors. It didn't matter to us, in fact, we all felt similarly pleased that no-one ever suggested the windows be touched, apart from to open them. A vase of sunflowers seemed to permanently decorate the windowsill – I guess they must have been plastic. There was no kitchen table. And we loved it.

The whole house exuded calm, and for two weeks of each year we usually had absolutely no problems or disagreements. This year though, we decided to have a change from our usual lazing, reading and swimming, and to hire a boat for mackerel fishing. The four of us: Angelo, Kary, the Doctor and I, all of us turning various shades of sun-tanned brown, all of us calm and happy, would board the "Wendy Jane" with no apprehension whatsoever.

When we arrived at the harbour, greasy with sun tan lotion and loaded with bags full of picnic, a local young man greeted us: James. In the small village where everyone knew everyone, we had seen James doing odd jobs, always busy - as working people always seem to be to fifteen year olds - but he was always ready to stop and have a chat about those insignificant, maybe traditionally British talking points: the weather, football and such like. We knew James well enough to like him, at the time I estimated him to be an ancient 30 something, but we were pleased when we saw he would be our captain. Kary and I giggled our way unsteadily onto the vessel which rocked gently beneath us and which appeared to me to be nailed and screwed and roped together in such a clever, yet precarious way. Close to, amazement was fuelled by youth I suppose at the intricacies of the wooden fenders, splintery to the touch and so near to rotten yet still strong. Through the door I could clearly see the dials, knobs and wheels of the navigation equipment set symmetrically in a handsome walnut surround, and there, stuck with a drawing pin, flapping lazily was a calendar displaying Miss August. Miss August. Semi clad and pouting with over-rouged lips and huge hoiked up silicone breasts only just concealed by lacy white lingerie, blonde hair, artificially coloured and curled, placed artistically around her shoulders; strangely curved spine resulting in an unnatural lazy s-bend of a body. Strange to think she was usually the only companion to James who stood coolly in silhouette, fiddling with some paperwork, concentrating elsewhere. A Polaroid camera swung gently from a hook, well worn and a little scratched, its worn out strap replaced with a piece of knotty string. I imagined

James taking spontaneous photographs of the choppy sea, or arty shots of happy passengers landing a big one and selling them at extortionate prices to the unsuspecting punters. I imagined James to be a jack of all trades and at that moment I envied him. Oh to be the captain of such a boat, I remember thinking, what fulfilment in knowing how to use those levers and switches, to be able to control such a craft through storms and clear waters. To have such steady, strong hands and keen judgement. To feel Miss August's sizzling breath on the crest of each wave. All this and to know how fast and how far just appeared to me to be the most satisfying act – an act so cerebral, maybe transcendental - knowing, not that you had completed the journey safely, but that the crew and passengers had depended on you to see them safely to the end of their voyage, that they had relied on you entirely with a reliance that was tangible. I could have been responsible for the most heinous crime, but that one single act, the act of captaining this seemingly unsafe craft, would expunge all that had gone before. I wished I was James. I wished I could take those snapshots for him.

Such was the passion of my teenage thinking.

Shaken from my teenage reverie by gritty exhaust fumes which were already throbbing lazily from the old diesel engine, I coughed dryly as they caught in my throat, but mostly for dramatic effect, knowing it would make Kary and Angelo snigger, further forging the ether of our relationship. I felt I had reached the pinnacle of happiness and as we shoved our way through the calm sea I can remember noticing Kary's wistful expression, her face unusually totally exposed as the sea breeze pushed her wispy hair into a fluttery brown wake. Within minutes, it appeared to me, we were way out to sea and the coast looked like a picture post card view. Up to that point I had thought those views were almost entirely fictional, touched up by avaricious photographers. Looking at that view from a distance was the first time I recall realising all was never as it appeared.

I don't know exactly what happened next but I do remember James saying something like "Here's good" and cutting the engine so that the boat came to a halt. The lack of forward movement seemed to abruptly emphasise the rocking, tilting, swaying motion of the craft and that picture postcard horizon appeared and disappeared with a predictability which began to feel uncomfortable to me. All around me, everyone was excitedly getting on with organising the fishing equipment; James, busy instructing; Kary, listening intently and following each instruction carefully; Angelo, squinting against the sunlight and not really getting it, but having a go; the Doctor, watching interestedly with arms folded. Me. I sat, gripping the splintered bench seats, feeling an uncertainty fuelled by fear and growing, cloying nausea. Each time the Wendy Jane rose and fell, my stomach wrenched and twisted. Closing my eyes made it worse. Keeping my eyes open confirmed the inevitable. I felt at once sick and angry – we were not in the grip of a storm, the sea was calm. In reality, we were probably hardly moving at all. No one else was feeling this as I was – or so it seemed. What was the matter with me? In a moment of clarity, I thought it best to announce what was imminently going to happen, and, rising from my seat said "going to be sick" just before actually being violently sick both in and out of the boat. It is amazing how strong those so-called "sea breezes" are

– this one succeeded in lifting some of the contents of my stomach and blowing them back into the boat, splattering Kary's bare legs and arms with that orange-and-cream mucosa that always seems so profuse and pungent as to be encapsulated in the word "vomit".

You know the phrase "stark, staring mad"? This is the most effective way of describing Kary's reaction. Unfazed by the fact that I was still in the process of being sick, and with the wonders of nature continuing to endow her with my partly digested breakfast, Kary, rather heroically, set about assaulting me both physically and verbally. I remember thinking how creative her language had become, if a little Americanised: "You stupid frigging creep!" She yelled whilst pummelling my back with her fists as I tried desperately to ensure that no further acts of nature could force me to share my bodily fluids with Kary. Only with Angelo and the Doctor restraining her would she stop her onslaught, whilst I, drained and dopey, flopped like a rag doll onto the bench seat and cried.

James was very efficient of course. He instantly took control and led me by the elbow into what he called his "captain's cabin", whispering placatory comments into my ear and sitting me down on his tatty but comfortable padded seat so that, together with Miss August, we made some obscure maritime threesome. "Have a rest for a minute. Here." He passed me a bottle of mineral water, "Sip this. I'll go and sort the others out and then I'll be back." I nodded benignly; thinking how that "oi" sound he used instead of "I" made him appear kind to my childish ears. Funny how a person's accent can affect your perception of them, I thought, taking a reluctant sip of the sun-warmed bottled water. I sniffed back my own salty tears and bile, feeling embarrassed and glad to be separated from everyone else. Outside, order was only slowly being restored, and through misty tearfulness and the murky glass of James' "cabin" I could make out, as if I was watching it on a tv screen, what was to become a firm memory: Kary being restrained by both James and the Doctor, stubbornly still enraged, and through the aftermath of her temper, everyone but me missing Angelo struggling to haul something in – something on the end of his fishing line which resisted and fought. It seemed to me that the more Angelo fought back, the more his puny teenage frame braced itself so that his sinewy small biceps strained and his skinny jaw clenched, the more whatever it was on the end of the line wriggled and tried to hold on to life. As Angelo battled with his catch, James and the Doctor continued to battle with Kary who equally clawed her rage at them so that they were completely unaware of Angelo's impending success. Simultaneously, both Angelo and James seemed to take on the stance of action hero in their separate plots – Kary seemed to be restrained and calmed almost at once as James firmly held her hands down by her sides, saying something close to her face which made her eyes first question and then calm and flicker a flattered smile. And Angelo, slipping backwards in a flourish of energy, hauling a vigorous, silvery brown mackerel onto the deck so that the slap of fish on wood rechecked a box in everyone's head, bringing them back to their individual realities. We all watched from our various vantage points as the fish flopped and twisted, drowning in oxygen, determinedly attempting to hold on to some form of life, flapping its gills and eventually settling on uneven death spasms which enabled James to scoop it up in his huge brown hands.

Of course, great congratulations were instantly bestowed upon Angelo, who beamed a great smile amidst forceful back patting and congratulatory arm-thumping. For a split second, Angelo glanced towards me in the cabin and we caught each other's gaze, but not long enough for either of us to acknowledge it because our attention was abruptly taken by Kary who seized and held the mackerel joyfully aloft, it still jerking a weak sign of life, and she dancing a bizarre celebratory dance as if she herself had been responsible for its capture.

XI

When Clive told Kary it was over, she seemed to take it very well. She didn't lose her temper or shout at him, and even though she was never supposed to see him again, she lent him her long black scarf because the weather was a bit nippy and he had to drive home in a Ford Fiesta with a dodgy heater. I knew he was going to do it, largely because I knew I had been persuasive enough during our meeting but also because he had arrived at our house that night with an entirely different demeanour. His clothes had been freshly laundered in a way that only a devoted wife could do; the smell of fabric conditioner was palpable (only a woman knows how much to over-use) and there were sharp, even ironed creases in his shirt sleeves. The jumper that he had to remove because he said the house was hot must have been a present from a family member – you know the sort, ill-fitting, patterned, hand-knitted. After he had left, Kary made us all some tea and we talked about work and the weather and then she went up to bed. Angelo and I talked behind her back for an hour or so. I sniggered behind my hand a lot, telling Angelo that it had been my doing that Clive had dumped Kary. Angelo listened intently, laughing in all the right places, and then we went to bed. Upstairs though, we could hear Kary's sobs resonating through the ceiling, down the walls and into the floorboards of our room. We lay motionless, listening to each hacking howl, feeling Kary's utter grief impregnating us both. Eventually, I could bear it no longer – that resentful sense of what was right kicked in and I put on one of Angelo's tee-shirts, determined to at least stop her from keeping us awake. The hallway seemed damp-cold with Kary's tears and as I climbed the stairs to her attic room, I felt a sense of impending doom mixed with a cold fear that only Kary could invoke. I tapped with loose knuckles on her door. She probably couldn't hear, I doubt whether she would have expected anyone to have disturbed her. I wrestled with the idea of leaving her alone, but then I tapped again, perhaps a little louder and the sobbing suddenly stopped like someone had flicked off a tape machine. So I opened the door and walked in.

Her room was a mess. Clothes, shoes and scraps of paper littered the floor. Upturned perfume bottles and well-thumbed magazines lay untidily on top of dressing tables and piles of clothes. Kary lay, curled like a foetus, on the unmade bed. Her eyes were mad wide as she tried to focus and I crept into the darkness that was her room like a burglar.

"Kary." I whispered, "Kary, it's me."

She was completely motionless on her bed. In the background, stuck on her walls, rather bizarrely, were pictures of pop stars from boy bands who grinned back at me, goading me on, their stupid toothy smiles posing at no-one.

"Kary." I whispered again, "Kary."

Somewhere outside someone's security light flashed on and the brown curtains cast a flickering shadow over the room. By this time, I was sitting on Kary's bed. For a moment we looked at each other in the sepia crudeness and I was pleased with myself that I had, comparatively fearlessly, got this far. Then, after a while, Kary, without moving said "I can't believe him. I can't believe what he said to me. After all we've been through. We were going to have a *baby*. We were a *couple*." She was incredulous. Her intonation was unusual, questioning as if she needed me to periodically confirm that I couldn't possibly have any idea what she was going through. As a matter of fact of course, I didn't know how she was feeling; I had only ever seen her relationship with Clive as a source of amusement for me and a pointless waste of time for her. Suddenly, she dropped her head onto my shoulder and the darkness in the room made the buttery smell of her hair even more pungent. So as she yielded to me and sobbed Angelo's tee-shirt soaking wet, the only thing I could think of to say was "Kary, Kary," and, stroking her lardy face like a mother, "there's plenty more fish in the sea".

XII

My teenage memory of the mackerel fishing trip is a significant one. It replayed itself in my mind frequently, and at the time, I didn't know why.

After Angelo landed the fish and Kary had been calmed and the excitement seemed to have settled, James returned to where I was sitting, alone, and asked if I was alright. I was grateful that he remembered me, I liked him. Despite the fact that unwelcome damp patches on my shorts and top were warming up in the heat making we ever-more aware of my own sour stench, I didn't feel embarrassed, in fact I felt comfortable. I was a little girl again, my feet swinging a couple of inches off the ground, on a too high seat, my hands captured under my thighs and my face bright with a toothy grin.

"Sorry" I said, really feeling sorry.

James was getting something from a small cupboard and I could see that he was smiling. He turned to look at me and it was at that moment that I noticed it. In the background, the sea was calm and greenish and out on the horizon was the outline of a white sailing boat which could have been drawn on for effect against the cloudless blue sky. What I noticed though, what came at me out of the silhouetted outline was James' face, and although it was a face I had seen before, although it held an expression of appropriate concern, a good looking face with sparkling eyes and a straight, strong nose, what came at me out of the silhouetted outline were James' lips. Lips as familiar as my own.

"How're you feeling now little lady?" Speaking emphasised them more of course, their colour, their shape, their proportions and as he mouthed those kindly words, the vowels which stretched and contracted them, the sounds which danced around that liver-red pre-raphaelite over-bite, this mix of sound and visual represented something I couldn't quite comprehend. I found myself peeling my right hand from underneath my thigh, almost involuntarily. My fingers were hot, sticky, meaty smelling from sweat and so on. I surprised myself by running my fingertips along James' upper lip – up until that point it had never been a habit of mine to touch comparative strangers in any way at all, let alone so intimately as this. I revelled in the touch of his skin. His lips felt dry and full, like a broken segment of a tangerine. They were warm and pliable and as my finger slowly moved across them, a drop of his hot spittle dampened my finger, and I smeared it across the inside of his lips. I felt as if my finger was disappearing into his face, as if one of us was morfing into the other, and suddenly I didn't know where he stopped and I began and when I moved my finger away, it – his lip - sprang back into that bulging beautiful shape. James didn't move. He didn't blink. He didn't even seem to be breathing - maybe I was breathing for him or maybe he was just amazed at what I was doing. It was like examining a familiar picture and it was like the realisation of something that had never previously occurred to us, something that anyway, we would have dismissed as an impossibility, but it was dawning simultaneously on us both. If what I suspected was true, it opened up so many questions that it was almost best left alone. My reflection in his dark eyes revealed a convex replica of his own, and, in the background, the sea was calm and a frothy wake was disappearing into a pattern of waves which gently rocked our boat. James was the first to break the loop of silence. Without blinking, he leaned away from me and, searching my face with his eyes as I was searching his, said quietly "You're a very pretty girl."

Such an obviously narcissistic comment could only be met with the beginnings of hysterics from me and I spluttered saliva in a spray onto James' face. Without thinking, and now into a new repertoire of behaviour, I grabbed the swinging camera, pointed it at James and clicked a photograph of his face. In surprise, he too began to laugh – I wasn't sure whether it was at me or at the situation and our laughter chorused simultaneously so that at the commotion I suppose, and as if on cue, the Doctor burst through the cabin door. She was sweating, pink and had an expression similar to Oscar Wilde: serious, jowly and distinctly affected by gravitational pull. She was keen to know what was going on and as she questioned us, her eyes moved beadily from me to James and back to me again, and we stopped laughing. Part of me was wondering why the Doctor seemed so agitated, I had never seen her so flappy. I could feel the connections in my brain start to fire and in my mind, my creative, fertile, hungry mind, a feeling started to grow. As all this was happening, the old camera had spat out the snapshot which had snagged on my shorts and was slowly developing. The Doctor noticed it before I did and after calmly asking again what was going on, she retrieved the still-developing photograph and the camera from my lap. Dimpled fat in her upper arms was tanning an even brownish orange and for what seemed like a long time she appeared to be analysing the image I had taken, her eyes flicking from left to right like a laser printer but the rest of her face unmoving, suspended in the moment. Then, without a word, she turned on the flat heels of her holiday flip-flops and left the cabin, taking both the photograph and the camera with her.

Some time later on the way back home, all of us silent for different reasons, I saw the white glossy edge of the photograph sticking out of the Doctor's handbag which had been dumped, open, together with James' camera in the front passenger footwell of the car. Kary's lobster pink legs now and then obscured the view but from my vantage point in the back seat next to Angelo, I could just about make out the image of the curve of James' chin, and as I strained forward, craning a little to the right, those lips, just about to smile, were clearly visible. As she stretched her legs out, Kary absent-mindedly knocked the battered camera. It was certainly an old model – grey, scratched and oversized. Wordlessly, the Doctor pointed to it and Kary reached down and lifted it up, turning it in her hands, examining it cursorily. Then suddenly she snorted in half-laughter, "Hey!" she said, reading closely some small, faded print from somewhere on the camera casing, "it says here 'If eye contact occurs, quickly wash the area with plenty of water and…" and here she snorted loudly, "…see a doctor!"

XIII

Exactly a week after Clive and Kary had gone their separate ways, I arrived home and a strange man was sitting at our kitchen table. He was smoking a cigarette and reading a newspaper. His left hand was curled around a mug usually used by me for tea, which, I noted with agitation, was currently half-full with muddy looking coffee. The forefinger of his right hand was moving slowly horizontally across the lines of print on the page and his head was tracing a similar line as if he was either reading something with great concentration or was too stupid to read properly. As I approached him, he seemed not to realise anyone else was in the room and I could hear his whispered reading of the racing page. I deduced that he was, in fact, too stupid to read properly. Loudly I flicked on the kettle and thumped a different mug from the cupboard onto the work surface. This stirred him from his studies and he turned to look at me, eyebrows at first knitted in irritation, then softened with embarrassment. I looked at him blankly. He should speak first, I decided.

"Oh…hi…" half a smile, very nervous, and then back to reading the newspaper.

A sense of profound irritation overwhelmed me. Oh, hi? Who was this man? What was he doing reading the racing pages, loudly, in our kitchen?

"Ex*cuse* me," I said, emphasising the "*cuse*" in a way I had heard Kary do many times to signal my impatience. Then I rounded on him, sitting opposite, in Angelo's chair, "Who *are* you?" I knew I sounded intimidating, but felt totally justified. This was our house and strangers were not welcome. The man straightened and his face reddened. I noticed he wore overalls with an emblem of some kind on the pocket. It looked familiar but I just couldn't place it. One of his ears was pierced and a heavy gold earring was making the lobe sag unattractively. Hastily, and rather disgustingly I thought, he threw his cigarette butt into the remains of the coffee. It fizzed weakly and gave off a final, defiant aroma of dying tobacco and the man smiled feebly in a kind of apology. The jewellery looked out of place on him. His closely shaven hair, pallid skin and sunken eyes betrayed a less than respectable past and he seemed to be searching for an answer to my question. Judging from his reading skills, this might have taken some time, so I thought I'd better help him.

"Do you know this is my house?" I said, actually rather unhelpfully, "and it would be nice to know why a strange man was sitting in my kitchen."

Embarrassed laughter from the man who said, with great apparent understanding of my dilemma, "Oh, god, yes,yes, I see your point no probs, like. I'm Kev from the satellite company? I came to fix your dish like, and your house-mate, Kary? She had to...erm, like, sign the paperwork?" He spoke with both a Welsh accent and a high rising tone which made me want to keep inexplicably agreeing with him. Yet, apart from the fact that I was pleased we had at last managed to get satellite tv, I still couldn't understand why he was sitting, so apparently relaxed, in our kitchen. Reading my inner turmoil, 'Kev' took on a more assertive tone, rose swiftly from the chair, scraping it annoyingly on the tiled floor and announced his departure, leaving me, his newspaper and half a mug of contaminated coffee. It was only when I heard the front door slam that I was sure he had left, and shaking my head in exasperation, I decided to seek out Kary to find out what had happened.

She was in her room, snoring, and I entered with a degree of trepidation partly since it was only 6pm. Her room smelt musty, oily almost. I flicked on her bedside light – the satellite tv contract, signed by her and 'Kev' was disturbed in the process, and I examined her sleeping face. She had been wearing make-up, most of which had smeared onto her pillow and some of which had been re-distributed onto the wrong parts of her face: lipstick across her cheeks and chin, mascara on her eyelids. Her hair was a mess of tangles and she wore a necklace – amber or orange plastic, one of the two. Her right hand was a loose fist hanging off the side of the bed, and in it was a scrunched up piece of paper, a torn off note pad which was easy for me to slide out of her palm. The paper was still warm as I unfolded it. Blue gel pen told me "Kev 07745 90908778". I looked again at Kary, at the dishevelled bed, the attempts to make herself attractive. I decided to replace the paper into her sticky palm, but in so doing, disturbed her and she snorted awake with bleary annoyance and with a dry tongue which she clicked agitatedly against the roof of her mouth. Taking advantage of her dumbness,

I said, "I've just been scared nearly half to death – some bloke called Kev was downstairs in our kitchen smoking a fag and speaking with a Welsh accent."

This initially raised a smile, but not for long enough and Kary was soon on the defensive. "Yeah? So what?" She sat up, mouth still re-hydrating, tongue swollen which gave her voice a drunk, lazy quality.

"Well, so nothing really," I responded moving backwards towards the door, "just wondered who he was and why he was drinking coffee out of my tea mug."

Another attempt at a joke to soften the situation might have worked, but didn't.

"Oh, just typical" Kary was coherent now, her face sinisterly lit from the side by the dim table lamp, "it's all about *you*, isn't it? Never mind *me* and what *I've* been through."

OK, I thought it was time to leave. But then Kary's voice dissolved into an indefinable sound, maybe a whimper, maybe a growl. Her chin dropped down onto her chest, which I noticed was uncovered revealing her small bare breasts. With a compulsion to cover her dignity, for both of our sakes really, I moved quickly forward and shoved the musty duvet up under her face and she grabbed at it and me with clammy hands. She was crying. Her shoulders jerked dramatically, robotically really, and tears popped out from the corners of her eyes and rolled down her face.

"I slept with him" she gurgled through the sobs and clawed onto me with such a fierce hold that I knew she had more to say. She turned her face up to me and though her facial features were indefinable in the useless light, the yodel in her voice was without doubt dismal: "He just came to fix the dish. I managed to speak to the Doctor and she organised it all." She sniffed wetly, "I saw him and thought 'why not?'"

I had to think quickly. Here she was again, laying herself bare and I had to be very careful.

"Well, what's wrong with that? You're a grown woman. You're entitled to sleep with whoever you want. I was just surprised to see him sitting in our kitchen, that's all."

I spoke gently, simultaneously stroking away a strand of tear-drenched hair from her face. For a long time there was absolutely no sound at all, and then Kary whispered earnestly without making any eye contact, "I just want a baby. I don't know why other people find it so easy."

This was just the start.

XIV

The summer in Devon when I was 15 was the beginning of some revelations, but not all of them as it turns out. You know what it's like to be 15, all those hormones and questions, but never very pertinent questions, and hormones which tend to get in the way most of the time. As a 15 year old you think you're invincible, you think you're always right and you don't like being told what to do. I was all of those things, and more. I was beginning to formulate new ideas about my world, about my life, but they were, of course, immature, raw ideas. All of us, Kary, Angelo and I, we were all big fish in a little pond really and we were happy there, too many questions would change things, change the situation, though of course what would be the problem with that?

So, three significant things happened during the holiday, three agents of change so to speak: firstly, my relationship with Angelo changed. Up until that point we had, obviously, been very close, we had, afterall, grown up together, but on this holiday, our relationship developed further. At the time, I thought it was all very natural, what with both of us having 15 year old hormones to deal with and the nakedness that sunny days brings issuing forth otherwise unencountered ideas, if you know what I mean. Now, of course, now I have asked the right questions, I realise that there was nothing natural about it all. Secondly – and I realise this now, I'm not sure I did at the time – my relationship with the Doctor changed. Finally, and inevitably, my relationship with Kary changed. Of course, the three factors are linked. You have to remember though, that as a 15 year old, I went with the flow because I was trusting – had no reason not to be - and this is what happened:

Angelo had been surfing and I was sunbathing in one of the coves. Kary was with the Doctor back at the house as she often seemed to be and even though it was the height of summer, no-one was around. The sea was sapphire blue and the sand shimmered like frost on the shore – all very romantic to a fifteen year old. I had been lying on my back and I sat up onto my elbows, squinting down my body to see where Angelo was. My skin was tanned golden brown and little blonde hairs prickled on my abdomen and thighs. Angelo was running towards me, grinning and looking like an actor in an advertisement for vitamin tablets or a health spa. To me he looked beautiful. He flopped down on the sand beside me, his chest rising and falling in joyous exhilaration and it seemed the natural thing to do to for me to lean across and kiss him theatrically on the cheek. His reaction surprised me. Grabbing my face in both hands, he kissed me on the mouth. A hot, wet kiss, a kiss that tasted sour sweet with testosterone, a kiss that made my insides feel odd, a kiss that lasted. It was me who pulled away, me who gawped stupidly at Angelo, me who noticed someone advancing quickly towards us. It was the Doctor, striding across the sand, her feet sinking into the dryness and slowing her down enough for me to alert Angelo. There was no point in moving, she would have seen us, and a million thoughts flew through my brain. How would I explain to her? What would she think? What would happen next? So we waited in suspended disbelief as she drew near.

What we expected, of course, was some sort of disapproval. The doctor was good at that, and disapproval was the worst on a scale of the approval-through-equilibrium-to-disapproval range she adopted. Disapproval could take the form of a curious facial expression reminiscent of her having eaten something bitter or unpleasant and/or a stiff talking to in a quiet but strict voice. We expected the latter and we braced ourselves. The Doctor's face rapidly came into focus, red from the heat and the sun, and we presumed, from her reaction to what she had seen us doing. Her step appeared strident, she was having to use her arms in the way long distance runners do, she leant her upper body forward giving a purposeful, assertive impression we had not encountered about her before. By the time she reached us, obscuring the sunlight and towering like a giant above us, I wasn't sure whether an extra dimension was going to be added to the scale of behaviour management which might even have included some physical contact – a slap maybe, and a hard one at that. The Doctor took a long time to speak. We couldn't see her face, she was in silhouette against the bright sun, and then she crouched down so that the skin on her pink knees stretched to shiny smooth and her face was close to ours and she looked at us. She may have been inviting comment or explanation from us but none was forthcoming. Then glancing from me to Angelo, she said earnestly "Well done, well done." Shocked and trying to measure the meaning of her response, I found myself searching her face for sarcasm or disapproval or annoyance, or anything. What I saw, however, was approval. Approval and something like relief.

So that was the beginning of a change in my relationship with Angelo and with the Doctor. When the three of us arrived back at the house following an up-beat, chatty but otherwise insignificant car journey in which the Doctor actually sang along to the Beach Boys on the radio, Kary was in the garden. As we got out of the car, and being swept along with the situation I suppose, Angelo grabbed my hand and we laughed loudly as we virtually skipped up the cracked slabs of the path together. The Doctor was laughing and trailing behind us clumsily carrying our greasy wet beach towels. We hadn't counted on Kary's reaction. Clearly, the prevailing levity wasn't lost on her, and she rose from whatever she was doing in the garden – examining leaves or something similar – and immediately her face took on the expression of absolute fury. She dropped her collection of leaves, clenched her little fists, straightened her bare legs so that the flesh took on a dimpled, empty look, and she screamed at the top of her voice. The Doctor's reactions were impeccable. She raced ahead of us, grabbed Kary tightly around the shoulders and rocked her firmly as she wailed like a dying animal. Later on, lying in the heavy silent darkness with Angelo in the bedroom the Doctor told us we could now share, I was simply consumed by a feeling of support and happiness. Kary's outburst was trivial to me at the time.

I didn't care if she didn't like what she had seen. I didn't even know if she understood. I was happy. I had just lost my virginity and ironically, as every woman in that position knows, the mere fact of the loss raises their status and places them way above any girl who still remains intact.

XV

A few weeks after the satellite man situation, Kary returned home looking sheepish. Her jacket was fastened up tightly making her look like a badly stuffed rag doll and her hands were jammed into her pockets. She stood perfectly still in our hallway like a rabbit caught in the headlights when she realised I was there. She seemed more bulgy than usual and I couldn't help my eyes wandering up and down her body, swathed as it was in the amber light emanating from the street light outside, noticing her discomfort and becoming curious about her shifty demeanour. Something was rustling, a carrier bag maybe. I could see the erratic movement of her fingers through the material of her pocket, almost as if she was typing a secret message on an imaginary keyboard. Irregular ripples from her pocket were the only signs of life. They made her look as if she had some kind of small animals hidden about her person. Without saying a word, Kary scrambled for the stairs and noisily clambered up to her room, slamming the door, audible breaths trailing in her wake. I had to weigh up the situation quickly and decided to follow her up to her room, largely because, even for Kary, this had been a peculiarly dramatic display of attention seeking.

This was, however, not an easy decision to make. Kary's moods were, of course, renowned, but I was physically and emotionally prepared with a swift escape route, and as I climbed the stairs slowly it was as if someone was turning up the volume on the sounds in a hamster's cage: manic, swift movements, quick wheezy breathing that only Kary could perform. Her door was ajar and she had flicked on an old table lamp so that a dirty, weak light was cast across her heaving back. She was still wearing her coat and her shoes had been blithely kicked aside on the floor. I stood for a while just inside her room, half assessing the situation and half voyeuristically observing the scene. If she saw me, she didn't reveal it and after a while, I advanced towards her feeling increasingly disgusted at her grubby room and her general dishevelment. I should say at this point that this was not an unusual prelude to communication with Kary. In fact, it was almost the norm. Until I would speak, I knew that I could, in fact, stand and observe her. In this game of conversation, she would not be the instigator of any verbal contact. So I took advantage for a while. I enjoyed the feeling of distain I was beginning to feel and even in the dim light I could clearly see that her thin hair needed to be washed and her face had that grimy look of someone whose facial cleansing habits were at best iffy. Her bed was unmade and I could see that she was fumbling with something so I entered her room and stood beside her. Stroking her shoulders gently, and sickeningly feeling the cold greasiness of the tips of her hair on the back of my hands, I said "Kary, whatever is it?" very nearly convincing myself that I cared. Kary transferred her attention immediately to me, which was unusual since normally the routine of communication required repeated questioning. Her face had a corrugated, doleful look, half lit by the nearby forty watt light bulb. She held a long rectangular box in her hand, the writing on which was impossible to make out in the dimness. Nevertheless, she rattled it like it was a child's home made musical instrument and just as I realised that what she was holding in her hand was a home pregnancy kit, with a look that can only be described as deferential, Kary announced that she was pregnant.

XVI

Some people believe that shoplifting is a crime, others, that it is a cry for help. I suspect it depends on the popular view of the time. Kary's view was the latter.

Towards the end of our Devon holiday, Kary was delivered back to the cottage by the local police. Evesdropping, Angelo and I listened through the kitchen wall, wide eyed with interest as the Devonshire burr of the police officer's accent explained how Kary had availed herself of several pounds worth of make-up and perfume from the village's chemist shop, and had then attempted to leave without paying. In the background, Kary's whining attempts at an interrupted explanation could be heard, but the police officer soldiered on, giving a list of exotically named beauty products "found about her person" and remarking on the abuse hurled at the shop assistant who spotted her. The depth of his voice vibrated through us and we tried to imagine the positioning, the proximity of one person to another in that little kitchen. We heard the Doctor calmly send Kary to her room and then Kary's sullen, deliberately slowed down footsteps on the wooden stairs, followed by a slamming door. A scraping chair – we assumed the police officer was sitting on it, the Doctor would never be so heavy with the furniture – heralded a lower toned conversation in which we heard Kary's sanity being questioned and the Doctor's composed, placating voice phasing in and out of ear shot with words like "difficulties…different…problem". Angelo and I exchanged glances as it became clear that the officer was swept into these various issues, issues about which we knew nothing, issues which ironically a badly constructed partition wall prevented us from being a part of. Overcome with brave curiosity about the unfinished sentences, the stage-whispered agreements, the strangeness of the situation, like a robot and without another thought, I straightened up and walked, as if nothing had happened, into the kitchen.

"Oh!" I exclaimed as if in surprise – it was as if my life, my body had become controlled by someone else, as if all this was happening to someone else. I couldn't wait to hear what I might say next.

The officer, his shiny buttons and badges well polished and his hat placed firmly on his lap, sat on the only wooden kitchen chair in the house. I had seen this chair before but had considered it may have been too dangerous to sit on so had never tried. Bizarrely I hoped it would withstand what looked like the considerable weight of the officer who appeared oblivious to the possible danger. The Doctor stood very near to the officer, maybe, I thought, ready to catch him if the chair collapsed. On the work surface sat an array of interestingly named and shaped bottles and containers. Both adults could clearly see me appraising the situation, and the goods, and they remained temporarily still like a tableau which could have been entitled "Misspent Youth" or something. As suddenly as if someone pressed the "play" button, the Doctor suggested I get a cold drink for myself and Angelo and the officer rose from the imminent danger of the chair and brushed imaginary specks of dirt from his jacket and trousers with his free hand. A girl can move very slowly when the motivation is right, and I don't think I have ever taken so long to locate two glasses, make sure they're clean, run the tap long enough for the water to run cold and then fill the glasses. So long was I that the officer clearly felt the need to fill the silence with some concluding remarks. This also gave me time to take a closer look at the swag. Not terribly expensive products: a couple of black waterproof mascaras, a very large red lipstick, an upturned glass container of skin foundation cream which was showing signs of leaking, three black eye liner pencils and a half empty bottle of "Desire" perfume with the word "Tester" across the front.

"Whose are these?" I asked, lifting up an eye liner pencil and turning to look innocently at the adults – there I went again, the words just tumbling out.

The discomfort this question created was enjoyable for a moment, and then something must have kicked into the Doctor's psyche and she said, "Kary took them from the local store, this officer has brought her home and we're going to take the goods back straight away." She turned to look at the officer and said "If that's alright." The officer was most keen to agree and if it had not been for the Doctor's insistence that Kary accompany him to apologise and promise never to do it again, he said he would have been quite happy to return the goods himself.

So, apparently, Kary was taken to the store, returned the goods, apologised, cried, was sent to her room after a long consultation session with the Doctor and cried some more. It was as if nothing more needed to be said.

Through to the early hours of the next day though, the various situations encountered by us all in that holiday played on my mind. Although the Doctor's calm, efficient manner had been all that we had been used to, I couldn't help wondering what event was needed to really disturb our strange equilibrium.

I decided to stop wondering and to find out.

XVII

When Angelo arrived back from work, I had already decided not to tell him about Kary being pregnant straightaway – it felt oddly meaningless, there was nothing to say except that Kary was about to present us with another situation. What was new in that anyway? So I listened to Angelo's account of his day. There's only so much about the cutting of Yale keys that a person can say, but one piece of information was interesting: a pregnant customer had fainted in the shop whilst waiting for her shoes to be re-heeled, and when her husband had turned up to take her home, it was Clive. Angelo said how well Clive looked, how compassionate and caring he had been, how he had virtually lifted the pregnant Jane into his awaiting car and how he had been so absorbed in making sure she was alright, he hadn't even noticed Angelo. More importantly as it turned out, so concerned and in a rush was Clive that he swept his wife away minus her newly repaired footwear. Angelo paused to sip his tea and then sighed and shook his head as if to say "what a day!" and to imply that was all he had to say on the matter.

"Clive's wife," I said after a while, "what did she look like?"

Angelo frowned and looked deep in thought for a moment.

"Tired, a little agitated, a bit pregnant."

You had to love him, but sometimes Angelo could be somewhat vague. I laughed for a second and then put the question more specifically, "Angelo, her looks. What did she look like? What colour hair, her build, her clothes?"

Angelo rocked back in the chair and gently slapped his forehead with the palm of his hand, feigning stupidity which seemed actually very close to the truth.

"Oh, yes, of course. She was just, well, ordinary looking really. Shoulder length brown hair, clean face, no make up, quite tall for a woman I suppose."

Even though his description was sketchy, it fuelled an interest in me. I really was keen to know what Jane was like. I wanted to visualise what a woman whose husband had been so terribly unfaithful looked like. I wanted to be able to imagine what kind of reaction she might have if she knew, and it seemed to be important that I could visualise what her face was like so that I could work out possible physical reactions. I wanted to know if she was aware of Clive's infidelity, or did I have the power of that knowledge. Did I know something so very important that she didn't? Totally ridiculous really. Almost macabre in a way. And as I was floating off into an imaginary revelatory scenario involving Jane (whom, of course, I now felt I would recognise immediately) and Kary and Clive, Angelo broke my concentration by casually saying "…and of course, we've still got her shoes."

Here, a description wasn't enough and I had a compulsive, some might say terrible urge to take a look at Jane's shoes, to hold them in my hands. There was no alternative, I had to have them and I knew that even though Angelo would resist at first, perhaps even quite convincingly, he would succumb to me. I knew the pattern of conversation, the word play, the thinking maze I was about to enter. I knew the links, the looks and the gestures. It was never difficult to enter into ardent persuasion with Angelo and even easier to win an argument. I knew that tonight I would achieve what I wanted and I would have Jane's shoes in my possession. At that moment though, I wasn't sure why.

Sure enough, Angelo put up a fairly convincing fight: the shop was locked (but I knew he had a key), the alarm was on (but I knew he knew the code), his boss wouldn't like it (but I knew he need not know), couldn't I wait until tomorrow? (no, I wanted them now), but they weren't his shoes to give, what if Jane returned to collect them? (If he let me have them now, he could return them tomorrow…) And so it went for a while, with Angelo's resistance getting progressively weaker until he could see no alternative but to please me. And he did.

Angelo's workplace was a shop in a thin mock Victorian arcade at the top of which a busy Italian restaurant bustled noisily, filling the cobbled space with the sound of clanking plates and the disembodied voices of competing diners. Heated garlic caught in our throats and made our stomachs churn. Night had fallen and a ceiling of darkness seemed to close in on us. Angelo reluctantly let us into the little shop with its burnt-rubber-and-sweat smell and its dirty cluttered counter which he cleared and lifted in one movement. Behind, Angelo deftly pressed the buttons of the alarm with his long, slender fingers and silenced the infernal beeping so that we were suddenly caught in the stillness which made us feel like burglars, and momentarily I snorted a laugh at the absurd situation I had put us in, and immediately clamped my hand over my mouth as if an imaginary someone might hear us and punish us for...what? Breaking and entering? Sneaking and peeking? Recovering and delivering? A couple, a man and a woman, walked past outside, engaged in light conversation, laughing and clip-clopping across the cobblestones. How ridiculous, I thought, to use cobblestones in a new shopping area. Let's face it, in Victorian times, cobbles were acceptable, but today, what with stiletto heeled shoes and fashion footwear, they're just not practical are they? I wondered why people ever thought the old, traditional ways were the best. Nevertheless in less than ten seconds the couple had passed the shop and their sing-song voices receded into the future, oblivious to us and what we were doing. I wondered if they would care but anyway I leapt into the shadows dramatically, really taking on the role of intruder and inadvertently noisily knocking a container of plastic key fobs to the floor only to snigger more but Angelo ignored me and scrabbled concentratedly in the dark, picking up and myopically examining several pairs of shoes. This act in itself was enough to fuel my hysterics and I began to understand how burglars felt the need to defecate in their act of burgling. Instantly disgusted with myself and my seemingly uncontrollable bodily and emotional functions and feeling the grumbling of peristalsis overwork so that nausea began to overtake me, I pulled myself together only just in time to be handed a pair of well-worn shoes.

They were old but good quality. Sensible is what the Doctor would have called them. Dark brown leather with a rounded toe, slightly upturned with age, and a block heel of about two inches. The brand name had long since been rubbed away on the insole and there were patches of wear inside at the heel, and toe shaped wear further down. Angelo had re-heeled and re-soled them so that both of these areas were unnaturally clean and sharp looking. There was a biscuity, old polish smell about them and when I slid my hand inside I could feel the undulations and indentations caused by the feet that had worn them. I ran my fingers across diagonal serrations on the new heel but even in this diminished light you could clearly see the reason for their repair, that wear had taken place on the outside edge of the heel as if whoever walked in these shoes preferred, or was forced, to tilt their feet outwards, like they were walking on the peak of a mountain, balancing, desperate to maintain contact with a dangerous precipice, working really hard to stay upright. These were old, trusted shoes and they were being re-heeled to re-balance them, whoever walked in them had decided not to walk on the edge any more, they were going to walk straight and even. Angelo watched me as I examined them and I felt compelled to congratulate him on his handy work. And then suddenly, it all seemed so clear to me. Angelo needed to return the shoes to their owner like the conscientious cobbler that he was.

Back home, we placed the shoes on the kitchen table as if they were a precious work of art or an interesting mathematical problem.

"Shall we tell Kary?" I asked it really in the negative, not as a suggestion, as a means of speaking and thinking whilst considering the consequences. Angelo looked at me, and for a moment I thought there was a glimmer of intelligence and that he would tell me absolutely not – I think I hoped he would - but before he could speak, as if on cue, Kary arrived in the kitchen. Carrying an empty mucky glass, she was heading for the sink. She was dressed in her nighty and her legs moved stiffly like a doll's beneath it. I had a compulsive urge to move the shoes from our table and conceal them about my person, I didn't want her to see them yet, I didn't want to explain. Having filled her glass with water though, she turned and her eyes settled on the shoes. At first, I thought she would just walk by and ignore us, and them, but she stopped in her tracks so suddenly that water spilt over the side of her glass and plopped onto the tiled floor.

"Are they yours?" She levelled this at me and I toyed with the idea of saying they were or to think of some other subverted answer to throw her off the scent and to give me time to consider whether she should be involved or not. However, Angelo, without hesitation said "No, they're Jane's."

Desperately, I was thankful for the popularity of certain names and hoped Kary wouldn't automatically think about Clive's wife. This was, afterall, my conspiracy, not hers, but she flopped exasperatedly down in between Angelo and me and stared at the shoes as if they were a miracle appearing in front of her eyes.

"We were going to take them back to her." Angelo spoke like a child, unaware as they are of deeper more complex emotions and motivations, and I felt the need to slap him or feign a sudden illness in order to bide for time, to gain some control. Quickly I laughed and said

"Oh Angelo, you are a fool" my mind working overtime now to prevent the inclusion of Kary, convinced as I was becoming that she should not be allowed into this plan but watching an odd chink of recognition on her face. Surely the links were far too tenuous for her. Surely she couldn't work it out. Surely Clive was becoming a distant memory now that she was pregnant. And there it was, the distraction I needed. "Kary!" I lurched towards her, placing my hands on hers in an effort to surprise her into averting her gaze from the shoes, "I haven't told Angelo about...you know." I gestured knowingly towards her abdomen and then waited for her response. Kary's face softened immediately, and her eyes filled, yet again, with tears. "Come on," I was gently taking control, "let's go and sit down in the living room and you can tell him yourself." Success! Kary rose wordlessly, followed by Angelo looking intrigued and I said "I'll put the kettle on, you two go on through."

As they disappeared down the hall I scooped up Jane's shoes and put them in the cupboard under the sink. Job done. I felt inexplicably relieved. My heartbeat thumped hotly in my ears and I wasn't sure why I wanted to prevent the situation from including Kary but cordoning off this strange idea from her gave me a peculiar pleasure.

In the living room, Kary was by now engaged in animated conversation. She was sitting on the sofa with her legs curled under her, tucked under her nightie so that she looked small and crumpled. Her right hand gesticulated as she spoke like a bird drying off after a downpour of rain. Angelo sat opposite her on the edge of a seat, leaning forward, captivated by what he was hearing – and Kary was capable of unfurling information in a very proficiently slow way. Entering with the tea, I was just in time to hear Kary say "...and I am so exceedingly pleased, because as you know I have wanted for so long - so, so long to be able to nurture, to care for, to love something of my own. So, Angelo, what I have to tell you" and here her legs sprang out in front of her and she slid forward so that she emulated Angelo's posture and I resisted a mean urge to yell "SHE'S PREGNANT!" and to spoil her big build up, "what I have to tell you" she continued " is that I am expecting a baby."

When delivering shocking or surprising news, it is, in my opinion, best to say it and then pause. Silence allows the information to be processed by the brain and then an appropriate reaction can be forthcoming. Kary, however, didn't subscribe to this view and continued to bombard poor Angelo with due dates, pregnancy test information and medical facts that even I was finding hard to follow. Angelo's jaw had begun to drop and his eyes were not focussing on Kary now, they flicked about in the way that some people's do when they are trying to deal with complicated information. His rate of blinking increased and I noticed his breathing quickened. I felt that if only Kary would shut up, he might surprise us and have something interesting to say. Kary, of course, was oblivious and continued to deliver her delight using a fairly repetitive vocabulary of adjectives, "fabulous" and "wonderful" and, rather surprisingly for Kary "super" being used time and again to describe her general demeanour. As she spoke, Angelo's perfect eyebrows began to knit a little, his jaw tightened and his lips pursed. Oblivious to this, Kary's adjectival monologue looped on.

Sensing Angelo really did have something to say, as soon as Kary stopped for breath, I delivered him a gentle basic prompt. "So, Angelo, what do you think then?" By now, he was frowning and it gave him the look of public school boy intelligence. His physical position remained unchanged and he focussed steadily on Kary. There seemed to be a long silence, but it may have been only seconds and then he said "How are we going to look after a baby?"

It seemed such a pertinent question. Spot on the mark. Obvious. Logical. We were, after all, a neat, tidy unit. We had routines, responsibilities. We had equilibrium, balance. We were three big fish in our own little pond. The question in itself was so vital, so important that it jolted my own thoughts. The question itself, even its phrasing was significant because though simple, the vocabulary revealed our subconscious connection: "How are *we* going to look after *a* baby?" We. All three of us were responsible, yet Angelo didn't say "your", it was just "a" baby – literally an indefinite article like an intruder into our triangle.

In an instant, Kary was on her feet, standing as upright as she could, her hands already tight fists on the end of stretched and straightened arms, her body bent at the waist and her face only, I would estimate, a centimetre away from Angelo's.

"What??" she yelled, exasperated, "What right have *you* to question *me*?"

Angelo's reactions were quick and he backed away, leaning his upper body backwards in the chair, but Kary advanced so that their faces maintained an intimacy subverted by the fear on his and rage on hers.

"I can look after a baby perfectly well. Why shouldn't I? How *dare* you suggest that I can't. *You* couldn't because *you* are *stupid*. An *imbecile*. I'm not like *her*." Her pointed finger shot over to my direction and she backed away from Angelo, slavering like a hungry lion, her face and neck blotched red with fury. And then she turned to look at me. Both Angelo and Kary were looking at me. I felt my stomach fill with something hot and my head lighten. For a moment, I thought she was going to advance on me, but she didn't. She loosened her fists and seemed to relax, her face lost its tenseness momentarily and then she tilted her head to one side and took on the expression of bitter, cold resentment. So tight were her thin lips that they were barely visible except for spots of white froth in both corners. She didn't move as she said "Yes, you. You. What happened to *your* baby then?"

XVIII

I should probably say at this point that contraception had not been high on my priorities during that summer in Devon, and beyond. When we returned home, the Doctor reorganised our sleeping arrangements so that if Angelo and I wanted to, we could share a room, otherwise, we still had a room of our own. The shared room contained a double bed, a bookshelf with some of my favourite books, a set of drawers and a wardrobe. Now, of course, we have personalised it a little more and moved things round, but then, on our return from Devon, the Doctor had left a copy of "The Joy of Sex" and on top of the oak drawers and a crystal fruit bowl full of condoms. We weren't instructed on the use of contraception, we weren't told to read the book, no-one advised us about anything and we didn't ask anything but we revelled in the apparent approval we received from the Doctor and took every opportunity to "learn by doing" I was absolutely and totally in love with Angelo. He was so familiar to me. Everything, his smell, his touch, every movement or word I could predict and savour. Loving him was easy, but being in love with him was pure bliss.

We were left to our own devices. If the mood took us in the middle of the afternoon, we would go to our room. Some days we didn't get up until early evening, some days not at all. It was a time of great excitement and discovery for us both, and never once did we read "The Joy of Sex" or use a condom. Every now and then, I would look at the fruit bowl and the flat red packets inside it and wonder whether we really should make use of those compressed circular shapes, but the idea just irritated me. They would mean change to my perfect situation and I had no reason to want anything to change. We were an encapsulated unit. Angelo and I lived for a while under the illusion that nothing would change that.

As winter drew closer and the nights grew darker, we cultivated the habit of lighting a log fire in the ornate fireplace of our living room. It was an excuse for me to cuddle up with Angelo in a romantic setting and it also appeased our conscience about Kary, who joined us moodily most times. It was during one of these evenings that the first kernel of consequence presented itself. The living room was lit only by the crackling orange log fire and the spiky intrusion of colours from the television screen. My head was nestled comfortably on Angelo's chest and I could hear his heartbeat, regular and strong. The whiteness of his arm around my shoulders was converted by the minimal light into smooth tanned brown and with his other hand he played with my fingers lazily resting on his lap so that we must have looked like a version of ying and yang, fitting beautifully with each other. Kary was fully reclined on the other sofa, her hands clasped behind her head as if in the process of exercising but her stumpy legs were crossed at the ankle in relaxation. I can't remember what we had been watching on television, but advertisements interrupted and each of us simultaneously rearranged our position as if a hypnotic spell had suddenly been broken. I looked up at Angelo who was already looking down at me and kissed his lovely wet lips, teasing them with my tongue so that he yielded to me and offered his own warm tongue into my mouth. I squeezed my body closer to his and ran my hand along his chest and abdomen, feeling him give in and wriggle just a little closer to me. I could smell his face, spicy with warmth, feel his smooth boy's skin against mine. Lost in ecstasy and desire, I didn't notice that Kary was now standing close to us, arms akimbo, until Angelo's reciprocation faded and I opened my eyes to see Kary's animal profile against the flickering tv and firelight. I couldn't make out her facial expression in the dimness, but her tone of voice revealed a parental-type disapproval, not embarrassed, but an almost superior positioning, an excuse to prevent us from persisting with our inappropriate public behaviour.

"I'm making some tea. Do you want some?"

Both Angelo and I nodded, feeling guilty, as we were supposed to. When Kary left the room, we giggled like the children we were and Angelo stroked my face and whispered something I couldn't hear but laughed at anyway. He ran his hand down to my waist and across the waistband of my jeans so that his fingertip lifted my tee-shirt and I could feel the warmth of his flesh on mine. In the background the firelight was diminishing but a lively familiar tune and bright flickering images filled the room. Somewhere in my subconscious, an alarm bell rang, and through the exquisite pleasure of Angelo nuzzling my neck, still whispering indecipherably and the electric sensations of his warm flesh ever closer to mine, the words of the song on tv pierced my flimsy balloon of happiness and cast a shadow of anxiety in my mind. Angelo immediately felt a change in my demeanour and reflected my gaze so that our attention was focused on the advertisement on the tv screen. Jump cut shots showed a day in the life of a young beautiful girl, working, swimming, laughing in a restaurant with friends. The familiar song beat on and the voice over reminded us that "just because you have a period, your life doesn't need to stop." Connections in my brain fired up immediately. In the excitement of the last two months, I had lost track of my own physiology and suddenly, feeling stupidly panicky, asked Angelo what the date was. Naturally he had no idea and I knew this would be the case but hoped that hearing myself ask the question would either dispel or clarify my thoughts. Instantly I began counting inexplicably in my mind. The figures didn't matter. I wasn't counting anything. In amongst the detritus in a teenage girl's mind, there surely has to be an area where clear thinking takes place but I couldn't find it. I stood up and started pacing about the room in the hope that physical exercise would force the blood through my veins and clear my foggy thinking. I scratched at the skin at my arms in the hope that I would penetrate the layers of idiocy which were preventing me from making any sense of my situation. I began staring wildly about the room, desperate to find a definitive answer written on one of the walls maybe. Kary arrived holding three mugs of tea in her hands, startled into stopping short at the door, surprised to see how the mood had changed in the room since she had been there last only a few minutes ago. By now, I was physically in the room, but cognitively elsewhere. My thoughts had solidified and what had been a shocking fear only a couple of seconds ago was now a shocking possibility. Kary set the mugs of tea down on the small table next to Angelo and looked at me quizzically through the growing darkness. Gathering myself together, giving the excuse of needing "the loo", I left Angelo and Kary in the living room and went upstairs to the bedroom.

The centre light cast a dim glow over the chilly room. Rose pot pourri, placed in a couple of dishes couldn't quite disguise a vaguely sweaty smell. The bed was unmade and a couple of coffee cups sat on the floor gathering greenish-blue mould. I could have had a lie down. I could have cried. I could have read a book and had a think. I didn't. Instead, I reacted to an almost primal instinct; an instinct which drew me to look more closely at the room itself, its simple fittings but its contrived additions: the books, the bed, the furniture. Not once in two months had I felt the need to investigate what else the room contained. Sure enough, I knew about the fruit bowl of unused condoms and strategically placed but unread "Joy of Sex", but now I needed to know more, to follow some inexplicable clues. Drawn to the oak furniture – furniture I had ignored up until that point - I pulled at the metal handles and opened the top drawer. It opened easily and was empty except for an old paper liner and a dusty smell. The second drawer also contained nothing. The bottom drawer was less easy to open, the wood had expanded or contracted so that it caught irritatingly and wouldn't completely open. The drawer's contents skidded and slammed against the wooden sides noisily. I shoved it closed with my full weight thinking, as some people do, that if you exert force over an inanimate object, it will obey your next instruction. Stooping down, I pulled hard with both hands and this time, it opened further. Inside the contents seemed to run for cover towards the back of the drawer, but I scooped them out and put them one by one onto the carpet.

There were three things: a box of tissues, a mobile phone and a home pregnancy test kit.

XIX

Kary acquired the nesting instinct remarkably quickly and when the incredible urge to clean the house resulted in her rummaging under the sink in the kitchen for cleaning products, she found Jane's shoes. They were exactly where I had left them. Holding them aloft, she said "Who did you say these shoes belong to?" Still smarting from her outburst from two days ago and overtaken with a sudden urge to cause trouble, I didn't even look up from my book and said casually "Oh, they're Jane's. I was going to return them."

My change of heart was, I thought, entirely understandable. I was furious that Kary had mentioned my pregnancy after all these years. Even though originally I didn't want to include her as part of my plan and had wanted to return the shoes to Jane myself, to see Jane and maybe Clive, to remind him of his indiscretion in a way that only someone associated with it but not actually involved with it could do, to make Clive feel guilty, now I wanted Kary to be reminded of her failure. I wanted her to look at the shoes belonging to Jane and to realise that they were shoes she would never wear, that the feet that wore these shoes were loved by a man she could never have, that she had been reduced to prostituting herself with a stranger and still she wasn't anywhere near as happy as she wanted to be. This, I can pinpoint now as the point at which the animosity I felt towards Kary was beginning to get out of control.

I wanted to kill her but I'd settle for making her feel pissed off.

Aware that Kary's eyes were burning into the top of my skull as I continued to pretend to read, I could wait no longer for the series of questions likely to come, so I said, by way of concise clarification, "Clive's wife. Jane." And continued pretending to read, inwardly basking in the fact that I was currently at least one step ahead of Kary. I didn't care if she became angry or irritated, I didn't care if she wanted to return the shoes herself, I wasn't bothered if she didn't. I felt nothing but hostility towards her, nothing she could say or do would be a surprise. So when Kary said "I'll take them back if you like." I was delighted. A quick fast forward in my mind to the scene with Kary attempting to hand the shoes back to Jane and being bashed about the head and face with them made me smile and I said wryly "Whatever Kary, whatever you want." And continued really reading without lifting my head.

Angelo appeared to have forgotten about the shoes and I made no attempt to remind him. Clearly Jane had not returned to the shop and whilst I did not want to appear to promote the idea to Kary, I wanted to keep it fresh in her mind, to chivvy her along, just for fun. Kary had taken the shoes with her and I assumed they were in her room. I had to be cunning. I decided I would have no more verbal communication with her about this matter, that way I couldn't be held accountable for any problems that later occurred, so I wrote Jane's name and address on a bright pink piece of paper and stuck it to our fridge. Naturally, Angelo didn't notice it but Kary did as I knew she would. She was after all's said and done, easy to manipulate, and I watched in great amusement as, following the disappearance of the address from the fridge, she furtively put on her large coat – made even bigger by the addition of Jane's shoes unsuccessfully hidden inside it – and surreptitiously left, closing our big oak door as silently as she could.

XX

There was a lot of blood as I remember. But this is rushing ahead.

I was sixteen, pregnant and had been sent back to Devon by the Doctor. Isn't it funny how those glorious holiday resorts look so different in the winter? Our holiday home was now cold and damp. It smelt sour and mouldy and it felt empty. Outside rain drove hard against the white rendering and seeped in through ill-fitting windows and under old warped doors. Initially, I felt bereft, alone and afraid. The Doctor had driven me there and had said very little. Befuddled as I was, I asked her no questions, instead I used the travelling time fearing that even the sound of my breathing might open a vast chasm of enquiry that would signal the end of something important. So I kept totally silent in that car, choking back a need to cough and enduring numb limbs from lack of movement, desperate not to attract her attention. Outside, the motorway whizzed by in a blur of grey, hypnotising time and taking me away.

She gave me the key to the house and asked me to go in and wait then she drove away. I obeyed numbly. Inside, a weak open fire had already been lit casting the only light into the living room. Damp wood spat at me nastily protesting against the black still-cool coal heaped on top of it. Even with my hands only centimetres away from it, I could feel only minimal heat. I shivered and tried to obliterate fond memories of the summer here, closing my eyes and sitting with my feet curled under me on the floor, desperate to feel some warmth from somewhere.

When some time later I woke coiled into a tight ball on the hard floor, the fire had gone out long ago and the rain had stopped. I was still cold. Yellowy early morning sunlight sprinkled in through the privet hedge outside throwing mottled reflections onto the living room wall. Unmoving, I lay for a while watching the changing shapes and feeling a sense of depression descend like I had never experienced before. In the strange shapes on the wall I could make out a bird flying in a small circle, a sail boat bobbing along dangerously and through my blurry morning eyes, I saw Kary's face, smiling widely like she used to when we were young. Nausea began to rise in my throat and my mouth felt dry and scratchy. My big mute tongue moved lamely about in my mouth in an effort to kick start my salivary glands. When I sat up my brain felt loose in my head and my eyes hurt when I moved them. I stood up shakily and the mirror above the fireplace revealed a misty reflection of a person I didn't seem to know. Indentations from the carpet had embedded my left cheek so that I looked like I had contracted some kind of unpleasant skin disease. In addition, my left eye looked bloodshot and half closed. When I rubbed it, hardened green pus skittered down my face and I had to blink like an idiot to clear the residual mucus sufficient to allow me to see that my hair looked greasy and that black dots of coal dust had already gathered thinly along my hairline. I looked dirty but the thought of washing in the antiquated shower filled me with distain; cold water would trickle unwillingly out of the blocked shower head, now and then unpredictably shooting out grey-white limescale, meanwhile the soap wouldn't lather and goosebumps would form uncomfortably against my nakedness. I decided to boil the kettle and to assure myself of a warm wash.

I walked blindly into the kitchen, grabbed the kettle and noisily filled it with water from the tap. Clicking it on, I crossed my arms, grabbed the edge of my jumper and hauled it up and over my head. My bra looked grey in that overwashed way and as I glanced down, my breasts seemed swollen and beneath them, my belly looked more distended than usual. I touched my taut, smooth skin. It was difficult to believe that there was someone else inside me and I felt my imagination drifting off to Angelo and the summer we had here. How it had all come to be. The acceptance we had received. The room back at home. The pregnancy test. The mobile phone. Then behind me someone coughed. It was a nervous cough and it made me jump and throw my hands across my grey-white underwear and turn swiftly around. It was James who leant uneasily against the kitchen door, his eyes fixed firmly on the floor as if he had seen something he shouldn't have. Part of me was relieved and I wanted to run and throw my arms round him, grateful for human company, grateful that someone might care. Part of me felt agitated that it wasn't Angelo. For a moment, I just looked at him, wondering whether it was a mistake him being there. I wanted him to be the first to speak so it seemed like a very long time before he said "Are you making some tea?"

I don't quite remember how I responded.

It's only the blood that I remember.

XXI

Clive sat, quite literally, seething. His hair had grown yet he looked balder. His skin looked red and tight, his long back was straight and his buttocks were pivoted on the edge of the seat as if he was poised to pounce. His hands were clamped together tightly and his thumbs twitched seemingly involuntarily. In amongst his agitation, there was a peculiar sense of excitement, and anticipation. A cup of tea sat steaming on the arm of the chair – I'd been making one for myself when he arrived so pouring an extra cup was no trouble.

His arrival had been heralded by a terrific storm – lightening sliced through the sky like a sharp knife and great hail stones surprised us with their persistence. Had he not battered on our door I don't think we would have realised he was there. He really did knock loudly, a knock that could only be performed with a clenched fist, a knock that was not to be ignored. When I let him in, he entered our house so assertively he brought with him damp night air, a sprinkling of those hail stones and a demeanour that can only be described as pissed off, really very pissed off. No conversation passed between us, it didn't need to and somehow we swapped places and I ended up leading the way into our living room where he sat down, dripping defrosted hail stones onto our sofa like a melting ice statue.

Amused as I was at his arrival at our house, my heart was beating with what must have been fear or excitement or both. I felt like a butterfly trapped in a jam jar. Clive's face was still pinched, its muscles paralysed against the elements which were against him, a vein in his temple visibly throbbed. Outside the storm was relentless and hail had now evolved into torrential rain which roared against the window panes. Through the crack in the curtains, electric flashes lit white and the inevitability of thunder ironically lessened the tension, but still neither of us spoke. I toyed with the idea of saying something like "So, Clive. How are you?" or "So, Clive. What brings you here then?" but I didn't think it was my place to say anything and anyway, the effect of adrenaline was far too compulsive. I liked the apprehension. I was on a high and I wanted it to last as long as it could.

Of course I knew exactly why Clive was sitting in our living room. Kary had returned Jane's shoes and there was bound to be an aftermath. I'd been expecting it – looking forward to it really.

I decided that Clive must be the first to speak. It's a well known fact that the first person to speak is the loser, isn't it? So I didn't hide the fact that I was observing him, running my eyes over his sodden clothes and dripping hair, noticing how the steam was beginning to rise from his soggy skin against the warmth of the room and how his long thin feet in stained shoes were tapping alternately. A chilly smell was beginning to pervade the air and almost simultaneously, we both shivered. Shock at our synchronicity made Clive meet my eye and for a moment his face softened and I had a suspicion he might speak, and he might have done had it not been for a noise from our hallway. It was Angelo and Kary. That was it, the spell was broken. Clive shot to his feet, and leaving a trail of muddy wetness in his wake, rushed out to the hall.

Often, we arrive at where we think we want to go and it's not what we thought it would be. I had spent time looking forward to this moment. I thought it would be good. I had ignored what was happening to me in the present, or maybe enhancing my present with thoughts of the future – with thoughts of this moment. Fleetingly, as Clive rushed past me, it occurred to me that I had arrived at the moment I had been looking forward to, and that maybe having reached that moment, the disappointment at my own warped imaginings would be unbearable. Gathering myself quickly, I raced after Clive in enough time to see Kary being carried like a new bride through the hall towards the front door by Angelo. Turning from their endeavours and visibly computing Clive's presence, Angelo and Kary stopped. Someone seemed to press the "pause" button and we were all suddenly pricked in time, completely still in a highly filmic moment.

And then the action, such as it was, restarted.

Clive launched himself at Kary, grabbing her shoulders and shaking her whilst she sat in Angelo's arms. His knuckles were white and his fingers pinched into her flesh and lifted her away from Angelo's grip as if she was a child. I felt absolutely no compunction to intervene, even though Kary's eyes were as wide as I had ever seen them and the colour had drained from her cheeks. Kary's bare feet hit the floor with a jolt and, still gripping her shoulders, Clive lowered his face close to her's. His jaw was clenched tight and stringy sinews were visible through the pale skin of his neck as he advanced closer to her. For a moment, I thought he might raise his hands to her throat and tighten his grip, squeezing the life from her, but suddenly Angelo shouted "Wait!" and once again the fragile moment was gone. As if to confirm his request, I could see that Angelo was pushing Kary and Clive apart, thrusting between them and uncharacteristically placing himself in conflict with Clive.

"Wait," he repeated quietly, chest to chest against Clive, "I'm taking Kary to hospital."

Behind him, Kary had crumpled onto the floor, hugging her belly, rocking back and forth, crying softly. On the tiled floor, in amongst the shapes and predictable regularity, drawing a growing thin line which traced the evening's events, was a pattern of redness, dark and foreboding.

Kary was bleeding.

XXII

My winter in Devon: Mostly I was alone, except for James. He taught me how to light an open fire using damp logs and suspect matches. I read a lot. I thought a lot. I tried to fix things – people - into place. At first I felt blank, but the more time I spent alone, listening to the wind rushing across the garden and through all the cracks and holes into the house, watching the trees feign death against the touch of winter, the more time I spent alone watching, listening, the simpler it all seemed.

When, at first, it appeared I might have been left by myself, I was appalled. I cried rather stupidly, feeling wretched with loneliness. Suddenly my whole life had been turned upside down and the basic infrastructure of my existence was brought into sharp focus. I went through a period of neediness, convinced I needed everything about my old life: the house, the jigsaw tiles in the hall, Angelo, Kary and the Doctor. I sat weeping, thinking that all was now gone, miles away, was probably never to be revisited or relived. Dead. What I had thought of as just an ordinary life was sharply defined, at first, as everything I could possibly need or want, ever. For a while I mourned its loss. I starved myself of food and sleep as a punishment for being responsible for losing the life I was used to. Meanwhile another life was growing, part of me, and as it grew, so did my hatred and my love for it. Of course, I had never felt hatred or indeed love before and these materialised in various different forms. They made me feel a physical pain in my chest and limbs and they made me sick. But they also made me think. Hate and love were responsible for my actions during that strange time – but isn't that always the case?

The nights were getting longer, in fact it seemed as if there was barely any daylight and for a week I picked at the provisions which had been left for me and which James replenished. Sometimes I prepared myself a miserable meal and merely pushed it about the plate, feeling queasy and full despite not having eaten. Sometimes I just watched as the steam rose from a pile of beans on toast, feeling limp and dejected. My skin began to take on a greyish hue, and my eyes looked somehow bigger and constantly red rimmed from crying.

Then something happened inside my head, something seemed to twang into action, something chemical. It was as if some movement within me was forcing me to do something and for the first time since being in that house, I got up out of my seat and left. Outside the air was biting cold and the winter wind pinched at my face and the bare skin about my arms. I was completely aware. I seemed to be breathing for the first time, pulling that cold air into my body in great gulps, feeling the dampness around my eyes cool down and sting. My nose started to run and I wiped it on the skin of my arm, prickling my face with ferocious goosebumps. Dark clouds were gathering overhead and dampness in the air whipped through my thin tee-shirt, making it stick to my body but I continued walking, leaning against the wind, spitting strands of wayward hair from my mouth every now and then and squinting to see where I was going. I felt the cold but wasn't worried.

I met no-one on the way. The area was populated usually by tourists and only in the tourist season. Few houses and farms were nearby, lanes were unadopted and clumps of trees seemed to go on forever. In the car, of course, the village shops were only five minutes away, but it was a good, brisk walk to get there on foot. I seemed to have it in my head that I would just take a look around the shops. I had no idea what day it was – it may have been a Sunday or a Wednesday, in which case the village would be deserted. I didn't care.

The village was, in fact, comparatively busy. There were some fairly lame Christmas decorations flapping diagonally across the road, linking one opposite shop to another showing images of Rudolph and snowmen. There was also a Christmas tree with flickering lights and a precarious looking star at the top. A few cars were parked on the roadside and the recorded sound of children singing Christmas carols floated in and out of earshot. A couple of the locals took a double take when they saw me – and I can understand why, I must have looked a mess. I was aware that I was shivering, so decided to go into the next shop I came to, just for warmth, I had no money. It was the mini supermarket, the one we shopped at when we holidayed. It sold, at extortionate prices, everything you needed on holiday. It smelt of lemon cleaning fluid and toffees. Goods were stacked haphazardly and unpriced in aisles which positively encouraged shoplifting. There was a constant buzzing noise coming from somewhere, probably a fridge or freezer, and a transistor radio played quietly – not music, a man's voice, maybe the news, his urgent tone making it sound like someone was trapped somewhere in the shop. It was warm though and I strolled up and down the cramped aisles quite comfortably as if I was about to buy something, actually just reading names on tins, boxes and containers: baked beans next to cleaning polish, fire lighters next to hair shampoo. Without warning, a woman's voice shouted out "Are you lookin' for anythin' in particular?" The emphasis on the "r" sound and the pronunciation of "particular" as "perticler" shocked me inexplicably, it seemed so long since I had heard anyone's voice that to hear one so rhotic and unlike my own or Kary's or Angelo's, was a surprise. It stabbed me with the recurring thought of them, Kary and Angelo, and twisted the knife of doubt that they had even noticed I wasn't there any more. It made my heart contract with need for them and I let out a sob of self-indulgent self pity that we had been parted, that I was there in that shop with no money, no warm clothes and without them. Standing quite still, I tried to stifle any other involuntary noises, clamping my hand over my mouth just in time to be joined by the owner of the voice: the shop keeper. She looked familiar to me of course but I doubt she remembered me. She rounded the corner of the aisle in search of her customer, clearly thinking that a sale might have been imminent until catching sight of me, still damp from my walk and dressed for a different season. Her eyes scanned my body and I thought for a moment she was going to ask me to leave, and then she said "If you're lookin' for arrowroot biscuits, they're round the front 'ere."

I was thrown by this and furrowed my brow in confusion.

"A-rr-ow-root." She enunciated wide eyed as if I hadn't heard, but I was still confused.

"Come 'ere," she reached for my arm and I obeyed as if in a trance as she gently led me towards the counter.

"There," she said nodding sideways towards the packets of biscuits plainly marked as containing arrowroot. "Well," she moved behind the counter now, "I know how I depended on 'em when I was expectin'"

Agitation was added to my confusion at this. How did she know? Could everyone see?

"'ere," she said handing me a packet "take these 'ome with you, they'll 'elp relieve your sickness, it's a well-known fact."

I wasn't feeling sick, but I must have looked as if I was, so taking the biscuits from her, I thanked her, and in so doing, heard my own voice in the first time in a while, thick with cold and gravelly with crying. As I took them, I noticed a sign on her counter. "Top up your mobile phone here" it said, and I remembered with great hope the mobile phone left in mine and Angelo's bedroom, together with the tissues and pregnancy test. I had used it to call the Doctor that terrible night. She had programmed her number into the directory and I had wailed my test results at her as soon as I knew. As I left the shop, the falling snow and soggy cold could not distract me from the thought that the phone might have been packed in my suitcase.

I ran all the way back to the house, clutching those biscuits so hard that they were hardly recognisable as biscuits by the time I arrived back. James had just arrived and looked startled to see me – I can imagine why – and I ran madly towards him, flinging my arms around his neck, sobbing wildly, and for the first time, into his shoulder. Without a word he returned my embrace, miraculously unlocked the door with his free hand and we stumbled into the house together. Somehow I found the atmosphere of damp and extinguished open fires unbearably depressing, as if the mere smell held with it connotations of fear, loneliness and anxiety, as if one sense had unlocked a far deeper one in my subconscious. But something else was happening. James' embrace seemed somehow familiar. His skin was somehow recognisable and the feel of his hair was like the feel of my own. Memories of our time in Devon, of our day on the fishing boat were confusing me and I knew I couldn't work it out by myself but I was holding onto James and I wasn't going to let him go. It seemed like the series of recent events, now a jumble in my mind, held the answer to a question I didn't, until now, know existed. Without loosening my grip on him I whispered to James "I need you to help me." Only then did he draw away from me, looking questioningly at my face, twisting his head to one side in enquiry, pursing his lips – those distinctive lips – in uncertainty.

"Upstairs, in my suitcase," I started explaining, "I think I might have a mobile phone."

I let go of him and he stood motionless in the hall, his expression changing from enquiry to helpless curiosity. I rushed noisily upstairs and began rummaging through my suitcase, throwing the remaining contents out onto the floor and shaking the case until I could hear something sliding from side to side in one of the pockets. Thrusting my hand into the thin lining, I grasped and pulled out the phone. For a moment, the euphoria took me aback. I sat on the floor breathing heavily, hearing my own heartbeat in my head, looking disbelievingly at the phone. Then I pressed the power button and closed my eyes, hopeful that it would flicker on like it did last time and I could call the Doctor and ask her to come and get me, ask her to explain some things to me, take me home, get me away from this place. This time though, nothing happened. I pressed again, harder this time, instantly angry that technology was letting me down. Still nothing. A voice from the doorway, James' voice, said "You'll need to charge it before you can use it." And he gently took it from me like the child that I was.

For a couple of seconds, he seemed to be preoccupied with getting the phone to work, pressing buttons and turning it in his hands in search of a missing link. Then he said, "Battery's gone. You'll be needing a charger." Holding out his hand, he smiled and I stood up with his help. I wanted to hold him again, I wanted to experience what I had done a few minutes before, mostly though, I wanted James to help me figure out a puzzle which was formulating in my mind. If I couldn't get hold of the Doctor, only James could help.

Downstairs, James made me some tea and we tried to salvage the arrowroot biscuits. My mind was buzzing and I didn't know where to start. There was so much I needed to work out. I sometimes think now that if I had known then how close I was to an answer, I might not have been so keen to pursue the question. Nevertheless, I started a clumsy line of interrogation, a kind of immature teasing out of tangles which doesn't quite get to the real question.

"How old are you James?" I started, feeling for the first time a sense of audacity. James was surprised I think, then he seemed to accustom himself to such a personal enquiry and told me he was forty-six years old. Heartened by his ready response, I commented on how I had thought he was younger and we both laughed, then I asked him if he was married. He was. I asked him how he knew I was going to be staying in the holiday cottage; he told me the Doctor had contacted him and asked him to make sure I was alright. He had known the Doctor for more than fifteen years and although she hadn't said why I was there, he knew her and she had paid him in advance. He didn't think it was his place to ask why I was there. I felt a surge of agitation that James hadn't thought to press her, he knew us all so well, surely he would have thought it odd that such a close knit unit was split up. I paused for probably a moment too long and James must have sensed my change in temperament because he reached across the table and cupped my small, thin hands in his large hands and, with more kindness than I could have ever anticipated, asked me what had happened. It was that closeness, that sensation of being touched which so easily released the whole story in a tumbling flourish: our holiday in the summer, my growing relationship with Angelo, and, embarrassingly, the lack of contraception leading to my current physical state. I recounted my mobile phone call to the Doctor, the swiftness of her action, the wordless communication and my incarceration at the holiday cottage. Throughout, James listened intently, holding onto my hands as if letting go would have switched the whole thing off. When, exhausted, I had finished talking, his grip on my hands remained tight. I expected him to be disgusted or to ask me what I thought I was playing at or what I intended to do now, but what he actually asked was, I reaslise now, far more pertinent. Without letting go of my hands, very quietly, James asked "Why would the Doctor have sent you here?" and it occurred to me that I had never thought, never questioned her, had completely trusted her. Everything that I - that we all - did, we did because we had been led to do so by the Doctor. I was mute, I didn't answer but my lack of response didn't prevent James from carrying on, a look of growing wisdom and clarification on his face. Then, as if we had both formed a telepathic link with each other, I knew what his next question would be, a question I had never asked before, I just didn't know what the answer was. Looking at me earnestly, James leaned across to me and asked "What do you know about the Doctor?"

XXIII

Kary lost the baby. There's a small smudgy mark still in the corner of our hallway where a crack in one of the tiles must have absorbed whatever it was that Kary expelled. It refuses to be cleaned up and it serves as a constant reminder of that night. Still, losing a baby so spectacularly certainly killed the moment for Clive. At first, fired up and trembling with the power of his own rage, he was reduced to the role of aching lover at the sight of poor Kary, dark red blood seeping through her flowery skirt and dripping down her legs. He acted quickly, scooping her up off the floor and carrying her out into the stormy night weather and into his poor excuse for a car. Angelo and I watched benignly from the front door as the redness of the Ford Fiesta's brake lights flashed through the rain into the distance. Neither of us said anything but as Angelo slipped his arms round my waist and we embraced, I noticed the trail of blood seeping in between the tiles, spoiling the pattern, disturbing the uniformity.

Kary arrived home by taxi early the next day. Not surprisingly she looked pale and drawn. Angelo was his usual sympathetic self, ushering her gently into the living room and offering her a choice of hot drinks which she quietly refused. When she also refused food, we all sat down in silence. She was obviously still wearing the same outfit from the night before and the stain, a circle of around three centimetres in diameter on her skirt, was now brown and had visibly hardened the material so that it was crunched up and misshapen. On her feet were a pair of someone else's slippers – the sort old women inexplicably wear; bizarre footwear with two tartan tassels which flopped against the bright blue polyester; flat heeled but arched up at the toes; the sort of shoes you'd imagine an elf to wear. Kary's bare legs were goosebumpy with cold, and black, stubby hairs manifested in clumps as we all sat watching.

"It must have been horrible for you Kary," Angelo whined, "We were really worried about you."

Kary didn't register any response and I hoped Angelo would shut up and in an effort to encourage him to do so, I placed my hand in his and squeezed it a couple of times, partly to show support for his efforts, partly to let him know he wasn't helping. Fortunately he understood and offered me a conciliatory nod and we both looked across to where Kary was sitting. It was an unsettling sight. She looked shrunken somehow. Her hair was a matted mess of brown and her skin looked yellowish like an old apple, though that might have been the way the light fell onto her from outside. What was most disturbing about her were her eyes. Still moist from crying or sleep or whatever they had done to her in hospital overnight, her eyes carried a kind of madness with them. Pinprick pupils in the centre of those grey, grey irises. Even though her body was slumped in a lazy curve as she sat, her eyes, focused somewhere out into the middle distance behind us, flickered without blinking as if she was reading something upon which her life depended. Angelo and I were paralysed with anticipation. I hoped Kary would, without fuss, accept our outward sympathy, go to bed and sleep off her trauma. That way, Angelo and I could spend some time together, every now and then dodging into her room with a hot drink and a snack. I didn't want to hear about her feelings or about any details pertaining to bodily functions of any kind. You might think me mean or even cruel and maybe I am, but we are what we are and to apply logic to emotion is not only a waste of time, it is foolish in the extreme. Maybe that is the theme of this entire tale. Nevertheless, at the time I had a faith in medical science which I hoped was not misplaced. I had faith that Kary would be too exhausted to want a conversation about what happened. I had faith that some things are best left unsaid.

Faith, however, is believing what you know ain't so.

Kary's voice was remarkably clear though her mouth hardly moved as she spoke and I couldn't help thinking how much she reminded me of a ventriloquist's dummy: those doll-like eyes and that peculiar quality to her skin and hair. It could have been a model of Kary that we were looking at, it could have been an impressionist's voice we were listening to. And we listened.

"I feel dead." She said, "My insides feel like they've been stretched and pulled. It's like nothing I've ever felt before. Worse than anything is the emptiness. Of course staff at the hospital were very kind, if a little dismissive I thought. One nurse, I think she was a nurse anyway, one nurse said 'most women have at least one miscarriage in their lives. Losing a baby is almost an occupational hazard.' An occupational hazard! Why would she tell me that? Am I supposed to feel pleased that I am like most women? Does it give me a kind of feminine seniority, a rite of passage? Does it make me 'normal'? Anyway, they took me down to theatre. They said they needed to 'have a look'. Have a look at what? I didn't ask. I just trusted them to get on with it. It was the most odd experience I have ever had. The anaesthetist was very efficient and that stuff they give you knocks you out before you can count to five...really deep sleep. I dreamt about the sea. About swimming in the sea. Maybe it was down in Devon, I don't know. It was warm and I wasn't worried about breathing even though I was deep under the water. I felt as happy as I can ever remember and when I looked down, I wasn't me any more. I wasn't Kary. I was a mermaid, and all the other sea creatures were part of me, or I was part of them, and they were floating and swimming around me and smiling. Yes, smiling fish and sea creatures. And we were all swimming in the same direction. All going the same way, not being swept that way or being forced to go that way, just happily swimming together. And it was so beautiful and blue and green and so happy...then suddenly someone was saying 'Kary! Wake up' and I didn't want to wake up, I wanted to swim, I wanted to see where we were heading, where we were going. I kept my eyes closed even after the image of those creatures had gone, even when the warmth of the water had gone, even when I knew where I was. And I started crying. Great big tears rolling down my cheeks and into my hair. I could feel them. And I wasn't crying because of what had happened to me. I was crying because of what had not happened to me. I was crying because I had been brought back to a conscious world which has dealt me such a spiteful blow. I was crying because I wasn't that mermaid any more. And then I felt the pain. Whatever they had done to me in theatre was gnawing at my insides. I felt scraped and raw, still do. Then they told me to get dressed and go home. They had done all they could. It was then I realised I didn't have any shoes with me so they gave me these. Probably a dead person's shoes. I really wanted that baby. I really wanted that baby."

It was said in such a rush that all Angelo and I could do was listen. There was no need to use any of those encouragement tactics like nodding or interfering with questions. She was on a roll. It wouldn't have mattered if we hadn't been there, Angelo and I, it was as if she needed to say it, she needed to hear herself say it. And in a way, I needed to hear it.

Momentarily, I felt a huge surge of passionate pity. My own insides: my heart, my brain, everything twanged with a massively personal memory and it was unclear to me who that pity was for, me or Kary. I was aware that my fingernails were digging into poor Angelo's hand and the extent of my sympathy or shame or self-indulgence rose like a nausea in my throat and, despite myself, I had to speak to release a tension which I thought was capable, at that moment, of killing me.

"Kary, I know what you mean." My voice emerged in painful jabs, "I can remember so clearly…"

My motives for speaking were, of course, entirely selfish. Rarely do we find an outlet for our own self-counselling, and how wonderful to be purging ourselves of our biggest hang ups and self-destruction material whilst at the same time appearing to be supportive and caring of someone else. This was my moment and it was a moment I didn't realise I needed – that's the thing with issues, they creep up and bite you and you owe it to yourself to deal with them. I saw my moment and I took it, I knew Angelo would view it as positive, as a sisterly meeting of minds between Kary and me. But so concerned was I to begin cleansing my own insides that I completely missed the danger signs and even before I finished voicing my first sorrowful, self-indulgent thoughts, Kary was on her feet and was standing only inches from me. I stopped speaking immediately, retracting, retreating, repacking, and suddenly our roles were reversed: Kary was no longer the victim of nature, it was I who had only just begun to lay herself bare, who was the vulnerable one. Without a word, Kary drew back her slippered foot like a five year old learning to play football, and kicked me with such force that when that bright blue polyester and rubber made contact with my leg I felt my bones vibrate, instantly jogging that self-pity back to wherever it had been hiding. As if once was simply not enough, Kary drew back her foot again but this time I was ready and quickly moved my rapidly bruising leg out of her range and Kary, with the unexpected extra extension of her leg, lost her balance, falling gracelessly backwards with a thud onto the floor. Angelo was up on his feet almost before she hit the ground, his arm around her shoulders, already murmuring placatory comments. Kary was furious. Her mad eyes glistened and she scrabbled with her clothing like a dying fly in an effort, I supposed, to retain her dignity. Angelo, bless him, gently helped her to a sitting position, looking very serious and concerned, straightening her cardigan rather ineffectually. And it was then that I noticed something. Struggling as she was, it was to conceal something in the sagging pocket of her cardigan, and the more she struggled, the more difficult it became to hide the fact that it was there, almost like some divine intervention was going to alert us to its existence. With great bravery, and anyway in the knowledge that I was more likely to be able to move more quickly than she could at the moment, I said "What's in your pocket Kary?" Angelo and I exchanged glances and he reached down to retrieve whatever it was. Unexpectedly Kary seemed to deflate, to give in and she seemed to flop like one of the sea creatures she had dreamed about, in sloppy resignation. Meanwhile a look of intense pain shot across Angelo's face as he sharply withdrew his closed hand from her pocket.

"What is it?" My own eagerness to know matched Angelo's pain.

Unfurling his long fingers, there on his milky white palm, twinkling comic-style was a silver scalpel and, slowly escaping from an inch long wound down one finger was Angelo's red blood, shimmering against the sharp metal like a precious jewel.

XXIV

Truth was, I knew very little about the Doctor. She had taken care of our basic needs in a very pragmatic way. In fact, we had never known anyone else in our entire lives. Everything we had ever done or owned had been procured or encouraged by the Doctor. So much were our needs catered for that she even seemed to pre-empt what we would want so we never asked or questioned her about anything. So James' question threw me a little.

"I don't know." I answered, incredulous at my own stupidity, but the question set off a series of thoughts. How did James know her? I asked him and, leaning back in the chair, he thought for what seemed like a long time. After a while, he stood up and walked to the window, turning his back to me. He was still wearing his coat, and I could make out his breathing through the heavy fabric. For a while, I didn't think he was going to answer and I wondered if deep down I had never asked any questions before because I didn't believe I would get any answers – a kind of survival mechanism – ask no questions and you'll be told no anything. I was almost acclimatised to the fact that I might be told nothing, when James turned and sat back down. For a while, he looked at me, searching my face like he was trying to memorise it for later on. Then he told me how he knew the Doctor. As he spoke, I realised the reason he hadn't answered me straight away was he was trying to organise his thoughts so as to make it make sense to me, and to make it make sense to him:

"My wife and I met when we were very young, not much older than you are now. She was a real beauty. Gorgeous dark hair. I fell in love with her from the start." He stopped speaking and smiled reflectively. For a moment, in the way that young girls do, I tried to be one step ahead of him, to guess what the punch-line was going to be, and thought he was going to tell me he was married to the Doctor, that she had been that beauty. What he was about to tell me, however, was considerably more complex. "Fortunately, she fell in love with me too and I was amazed, I mean, me and this fabulous girl. I couldn't believe my luck." He paused again to gaze with dim contentment at me. A connection clicked him back to the present and he continued with a sigh, "Well, one thing led to another and the years went by, we got engaged – we did everything right, she was a very old fashioned girl and we didn't live together until the day we got married. We had a bedsit near the harbour. It was impossible to heat and it was too small even for just two people, but we were so happy we didn't care. We had each other. Every day I'd go out on the boat fishing or taking folks places and every night I'd come back to her and we just never thought we could be happier." He paused again and my adolescent brain caught a tragic edge to his tone. Surely he was about to tell me that their happiness was about to be broken in two, that she was a liar and a tart; that he came home from a hard day's work one day to find her in bed with his best friend and he ran them both out of town and never recovered from the shock – that the Doctor helped him through it with her counselling skills. He continued after a while: "We managed to save some money and we bought ourselves a little cottage in the village. By this time, we'd been married a while of course and, well, it seemed like the right time to start our own family. A child of our own would just make our lives complete. But…" and here he hesitated, searching carefully for the correct words to communicate to a fifteen year old pregnant girl, "but, we just couldn't seem to do it, I mean, we knew what to do and we could obviously do it, and we did do it, we loved each other but…but, nothing we did *worked*. We just couldn't seem to get pregnant. We tried everything: we tried taking her temperature to calculate when she was ovulating, we tried changing our diet because we thought we might not be eating enough vitamins, we tried different positions…" he stopped and looked with panic at me for a second then, wondering, I suppose whether he had overstepped the mark. I offered an encouraging smile, intrigued at how much female biology James knew and how easily he recounted. And he continued, almost confessionally, "but nothing worked. Every month became a nightmare. My wife became terribly depressed and I was powerless to help her. I was doing my best but…so we went to our GP. Well, in those days, you were just told to keep trying, to relax, to enjoy your childless days, that sooner or later you'd be a parent with all those worries and sleepless nights and dirty nappies. So we kept trying. But still no pregnancy." He stopped and ran his hands through his hair agitatedly. "My wife became ill, really ill. She lost weight and she lost the will to carry on, it was awful, really awful. So when I saw something in our local paper, not exactly an advertisement, more a request for volunteers, volunteer couples who were keen to have children but were having no luck, I rang the number." Here I stopped him for clarification. Volunteer couples? Volunteering for what? James gestured with a wave for me to wait, and he carried on: "It all seemed above board and we were so desperate, to be honest, we would have done anything. Turns out we were the only couple to respond and I remember we made an appointment and we had to go to a suite of offices in Exeter. We felt hopeful, proactive at last. The offices were plush with pot plants and what have you. I remember thinking how little my wife looked sitting in a big squishy brown leather armchair as we waited. I so wanted to make her happy. Well, we weren't kept waiting long. Who should be there to consult with us, obviously much younger then, was the Doctor." My mind didn't compute for a minute, but anyway before I had chance to try to work it out, James went on: "That was the first time we met her, at her fertility clinic. She ran loads of tests on both of us. Very efficient as you'd imagine, and very quick. In literally no time at all we found out why we couldn't have children." Here, he hung his head a little in what I suppose now must have been embarrassment, "I don't suppose I should feel it, but it was my fault, nothing wrong with my wife. It was my workings that weren't exactly top notch." He laughed nervously and the way he edged around the point using self-deprecation made me feel instantly sorry for him. This time, I reached out and took his hand. James couldn't stop now, "At first, I was heart broken. The thought of not having children, the thought of how I knew my wife would feel was…terrible. But the Doctor said there was this new treatment, and we were exactly right for it, and if we were willing to give it a go, she might be able to help us. Of course, it's not so new now, thousands of folks have had it, but we were happy to do it. So my wife had to undergo some hormone treatment – nasty really but we did it, then the Doctor took some eggs from her – we joked she was like old Farmer Buckfasts's wife collecting good eggs from her hens – and me, well, I did my bit by providing a sample for her." He stopped, embarrassed again, "and the Doctor, well, she made sure she chose good stuff from both of us but she had to make sure fertilisation took place by injecting my…you know…directly into my wife's egg – no chances taken. Well," James sat back, taking his hand from mine. My mind charging forward, I inhaled sharply. "Lucky for us it worked," James, comfortable now, sat back, "and we had our son, Patrick."

Listening to James' story and watching his face, his lips, I reached the only conclusion a teenage girl could; a conclusion based on a concept I had never before considered – a half formed, self-centred, startling conclusion: that somehow James and his wife were my parents.

XXV

At first, we thought Kary had stolen the scalpel from hospital with the aim of hurting herself. It can be more than simply depressing to lose a baby and we knew that Kary was prone to mood swings. Angelo's hand was bleeding profusely and he gazed forlornly at the wound. My heart leaping, and with Kary in a faint on the floor, I seized the moment to inspect both his hand and the scalpel. The cut was not deep but it was long and I suspected it was painful. I told Angelo to come with me into the kitchen and he followed me holding the scalpel like an unexploded bomb, dripping splodges of blood as he walked. Once at the kitchen sink, I took the scalpel and turned the tap on. His hand was warm in mine and crimson blood oozed out of the cut, appearing quickly like a string of little rubies across his palm. Something about the total trust he placed in me, about the warmth of his skin, the way his other hand rested around my waist, something about it all compelled me to do what I did next. It seemed perfectly normal and even now as I write it, I can recall only pleasure from what I did, in fact, the pleasure redoubles with the act of recounting it:

Angelo's body was pressed against mine, his hand rested in my hand and his blood leaked into a pool in his palm, tracing the map of lines and resting like a lake. Without thinking, without saying a word, I lowered my head and, feeling the sticky heat rising onto my face, I licked along the cut, tasting the salty, metallic warmth and feeling Angelo's fingertips stroke my face. Tantalised by what I was doing, I kissed his poor hand, feeling his hot, quick breath close to my neck now and knowing that our bond was stronger than anything we could possibly understand. When I tasted the blood that had collected in his palm it left a sweet, almost sickly tang but Angelo didn't take his hand away, on the contrary, with his other hand, he stroked my neck and the more blood that seeped out of him, the more I bathed his wound with my tongue. And I didn't close my eyes. I wanted every sensory experience from this. I wanted to see, close to, lines and envelopes and craters of his skin, I wanted to know every part of him. After a while, and reluctantly, I lifted my head and Angelo was looking at me and I think our expressions mirrored one another. I placed his hand on my cheek, leaned forward and pressed my lips against his, hoping he would taste what I had tasted.

Then Kary was in the kitchen with us.

The only way to describe what happened next is in purely filmic terms. Imagine this:

Long shot of Kary framed by the open kitchen door; slowly zoom into her face until close up showing an expression of absolute, red-blooded fury (jaw clenched, eyes narrowed etc.) Fast jump cut to mid shot of Angelo and I as we turn our heads in unison, noticing Kary is there. Our expressions change quickly from bliss to out and out fear. Close up of our hands, still held, jump cut to mid shot of Kary, advancing towards us. Extreme close up of the scalpel, now on the kitchen surface, blood on its blade already drying to a brown-red; a series of jump cut shots with hand held camera, close ups of our faces, extreme close ups of our hands, blurring. Transitions are very fast and the whole attack takes only seconds but the sequence seems frenzied. A long shot shows the obscenity of the event – arms, legs and heads flaying until the scalpel is knocked from the work surface by one of us and a tracking close up shows it gaily spinning across the kitchen in slow motion (add music here). The shock stops the fight and all three of us, in mid shot, gaze in a freeze frame at the sharp metal slicing through the air away from us. There is no sound. Switch to normal speed as the scalpel hits the wall and crashes to the floor, add the sound of the water, still running from the tap in the kitchen sink, jump cut shot to close up of the tap, quick jump cut to my face, tight with fear, anticipation and anger, my eyes flick to Kary, now unaware and confused; mid shot of me grabbing her and shoving her head under the tap; extreme close up slowly panning her squinting, spluttering, incensed face in the stream of cold, clear water. Quick jump cut to close up of my bloodied face, bloodied from all of us, as I hold her firmly there, smiling. Fade to black.

Later on I salvaged the scalpel. The blood had dried on it and it seemed undamaged. Kary had immediately retreated to her room looking like a drowned animal, shouting obscenities to us, leaving us to bathe new wounds. When I was at last alone, I considered what to do. The blade was incredibly sharp and in the wrong hands, this could be highly dangerous. The reason why Kary brought it home was a concern to me. Yes, she might be getting into self-harm, but it was just as likely that she intended to harm Angelo or me, or both. Turning the implement in my hand, feeling it readily warm up from the heat of my skin in that tacky, sullied way that some metals do, I made a decision. I decided to give the scalpel back to Kary. My thinking was that even she would not choose to use it against us if we were so overt with her. Keeping it or discarding it would simply brush her intention, whatever it was, under the carpet. The intention, in effect, would be buried with the weapon. By giving it back to her, it seemed to me, we would be making her face up to her plan and trusting her not to carry it out. So it was with high spirits that I knocked on the door of her room and entered without hearing her response.

To my surprise, she wasn't lying on her bed, she wasn't even sitting, she was, in fact, standing at her window, gazing out. She was naked and her back was towards me and somehow her nakedness didn't surprise or shock me. Her hair was still damp and hung in rats' tails. Her clothes, looking like she had simply unzipped and walked out of them, lay crumpled sadly on the floor. Avoiding looking at the dimpled white skin of her arms and legs and the creased grooves and bumps of her flabby back and bottom, I announced, as people inexplicably do, my arrival. Not expecting, or receiving a response, I continued talking. Very calmly and pragmatically, I told her that I was there to return the scalpel to her, that we hoped she understood how dangerous it was, that we trusted she didn't intend to hurt herself, or us, with it and that I would leave it on her bed in the hope that she would either throw it away or give it back to the hospital – surely they keep a track of that kind of instrument anyway, they'd probably need to have it back. Kary said nothing, but as I left the room I was sure her rumy eyes, bleary with tears of sadness (or something) flicked towards me and I closed the door quietly behind me.

XXVI

By the time I arrived at James' house, I was convinced I was about to meet my mother. Not quite sure of the hows and whys, I felt my heart thudding and movements inside me were not just of another being. Scientists refer to Simple Harmonic Motion. Ironically, there was nothing simple or particularly harmonic about the force of attraction to James' house. It was painful to me and far from simple.

The journey there had been short and cold. James' van was probably unsafe. The passenger seat was not fixed securely and jiggled disconcertingly and noisily from side to side as James snaked knowledgably round the thin, windy Devon lanes. The heater didn't work and at least one hole in the footwell allowed freezing air to whistle through, chilling us further. But I wished he would drive faster.

Like many Devonian cottages, James' was rendered and whitewashed – protection against the elements is vital in that part of the country. I could see that in the summer the small garden would have been a vast array of colours and smells, but now, in the winter, plants were limp and brown, hibernating in readiness for a warmer future. Grey paving stones made a path to the door, sloping upwards like a ramp. An old, badly constructed wooden fence offered some help as we walked up the incline towards the glass panelled door. A bright bulb hanging from a ceiling, shaded by a tasselled orange lampshade radiated peachy light down into the hall and that, and the smell of cooking inextricably fuelled my suspicions that only my mother could greet me like this. James walked on ahead of me, taking off his jacket as he did.

The hall was surprisingly long, dark and narrow, littered with what looked like metal bars and small wheels of some sort. At that moment, I wasn't paying too much attention, I was focused on meeting the family; uncharacteristically for me, the décor and general surroundings were way down my list of priorities and my usual observance of the visual was suppressed by a growing desire to plunge myself into a situation I didn't even, until that moment, believe existed. But it was clear that they were not well-off. At the end of the hall was a panelled door, powder blue paint chipped off at even horizontal intervals giving it a battered, dirty look. It was stiff and James shoved it familiarly with his shoulder to reveal a tiny old fashioned kitchen. On the stove a saucepan bubbled rather precariously and James rushed to turn down the gas, turning to me with an embarrassed half-grin as he did. I wanted to say "where is she?" but I just grinned back in a half-hearted kind of way and stepped backwards since there was hardly room for two of us in the little room.

"I'll get that charger for you," James said, and my heart sank as I remembered that was the reason we had come to his house – not for me to meet my mother at all. But I wasn't going to waste the opportunity and as he brushed past me back into the hall, I asked if his wife was in, said it would be a shame not to meet her now I was here. For a moment I thought James hesitated, maybe trying to recall where the mobile phone charger was, maybe for another reason, and I watched as he wrestled with an idea which might have been tinged with discomfort. I suppose he was in an impossible situation really, he had to let me meet her. Lying to me and saying she was out would have been silly because in my current frame of mind I would have questioned why she left the saucepan boiling – I felt I had a right to see her. So James nodded and I caught a familiar look in his eye as he made his way upstairs, it was a look of resigned compliance and I wasn't sure what it meant. Although I wanted to follow him, I didn't, I waited downstairs in their cold orange hall. Voices upstairs gave me hope and I suddenly started putting together a photo-fit of my mother in my mind: long dark hair, gorgeous as James had said, tall, slim, strong features, like mine, and sparkling green eyes of the sort that only she and I could possibly have. My lips, of course, were from James, at that moment that was absolutely certain, so her lips might be slightly thinner and pinker, but I felt that when I saw them together, James and his wife, I would be able to meld together their looks and their souls and inevitably come up with me.

It seemed to take an age for James to return and when he did he was alone. My disappointment was quickly abated by his cheery instruction to go with him and sit down in what was a comparatively warm living room. What struck me as I sat down on a well-worn sofa was not the range of colours in the carpet or the lack of tv or even the display of apparently thriving pot plants on the window sill, it was the books on the huge bookshelf next to me. There were so many of them and they were all children's books – not classics, not older children's stories, but very young, infant style picture books. Glancing across the shelf I estimated there must have been at least a hundred of these wordless hardbacks, their garish colours screaming out to be noticed. I contemplated saying something, asking why so many, but changed my mind in time to hear swift footsteps descending the stairs, pacing quickly towards us, the owner of them absent of the knowledge that I had already decided she was my mother; absent of the knowledge that she could have another child, a sister to Patrick sitting, anxious and nauseous, right there in her living room. The door rattled open easily and both James and I stood up simultaneously. Nervously I wiped the sweating palms of my hands down trousers, not prepared to meet my mother with clammy hands and the best I could do in the circumstances. The first thing I saw was her fingertips with short, neat fingernails, clutching the edge of the door. Then she arrived. Like the child that I was, I could feel my whole demeanour eager to please this woman and I inhaled a deep breath, trying unsuccessfully to avoid appraising her too closely on first meeting.

My recollection is that I made a pretty good job of withholding the real shock I felt. James' wife was not exactly what my imagination had created. There was no doubt that she was beautiful, her hair was the blackest I have ever seen and her eyes the creamiest brown. Not tall, in fact shorter than me and as she looked up at my face to greet me, she beamed the biggest, whitest smile I had ever seen – a smile that stretched her face and crinkled her eyes. Her clothes confirmed my suspicion that they had very little money to spare – the cardigan she was pulling around her plump body had seen better days and the hem of her long cotton skirt had come undone in places, trailing odd pieces of cotton almost down to the floor. But it was her skin that fascinated me. Shiny skin, the smoothest skin I had ever seen. And even though her smile creased the skin around her eyes, when she stopped smiling, not a shadow of wrinkles was left, no blemishes. I felt insatiably tempted to touch it, to stroke her face, and if I did, I suspected a greasy residue would remain on my fingers for a while. I wanted to experience the undulations of her plumped cheeks and the softness of her long dark eyebrows. Dealing with my own surprise was something I hadn't banked on. So sheltered had my upbringing been that James' wife was the first black person I had ever seen and, as further confirmation of my naivety I toyed with telling her so. I didn't of course.

Her name was Dawn and she shook my hand firmly – that kind of two handed hand shake which really is heartfelt and warm. She said that James had spoken about me, then she looked down at my swelling belly and her expression changed to one that I realise now was concern. She asked me to sit down. I remained mute and did as I was told. Her voice was as dark as her skin, a lovely voice, warm and gentle with that lilting tone that can only be interpreted as caring. Inside my head connections were beginning to close down. How could she be my mother? She was a black woman and I was white, it was impossible. In the background James and Dawn were talking to me, asking questions, and I was answering them, but I was trying to work it out. Somewhere in my subconscious a glimmering hope still existed. Relationships were being linked. Knowing the Doctor's relationship with James and Dawn, knowing how she had helped them to have one child, knowing how revolutionary the process had been, surely it would be possible to produce a white child from mixed parentage, surely it was still not an impossibility that James and Dawn were my parents. Surely, I thought, science could have been responsible for turning me white. By the time Dawn was leaving the room to make me some tea, I needed to absolutely convince myself that these two people were my parents. Sometimes faith can be overwhelming.

James sat opposite me and for a while we were silent. Warming to my own scientific theory, I asked the only question I could at the time, "would it be possible to meet Patrick?" It seemed the logical move. My brother should be physically similar to me, even if his skin was darker. Seeing Patrick with my own eyes would confirm the wonder of biology, of family, of ideas that were completely new to me. It all seemed so simple that when James hesitated, I found it hard to disguise my confusion. He didn't say anything, but his body language revealed an unwillingness; he visibly stiffened, sitting upright and averting his eyes from my face. His expression changed making him look older and worried – that was one of the things we had in common, an inability to prevent our facial expressions from exposing what we really thought. Still without a word and without moving, he looked down at his hands which played out a kind of unusual hand-washing ritual and for a moment I wondered if Patrick was dead and, rather selfishly, how exasperating that would be for me. On the other hand, I thought, if Patrick was dead, how wonderful for them to have an offspring they hadn't banked on: me. James sat for a while longer, contemplating his own limbs, and the longer it took, the more eager I became to know, to see even a photograph of Patrick. An unproductive silence hung over us until Dawn arrived with a tray of tea and noisy cups and saucers. Some people believe that children learn to be manipulative, but since I had very little knowledge of normal interpersonal relationships at the time, what I did next contradicts this theory and without a second thought I turned my attention to Dawn. "Would it be possible to meet Patrick?" I repeated in exactly the same tone as I had done before. Playing mom off against dad must be nature rather than nurture. Dawn's reaction was totally opposite to James', who noticeably twitched with what could have been nerves. Dawn unfurled her long fingers from the corners of the tea tray and smiling that huge white smile said "You want to meet our Patrick?" Then straightening up to her full height, she laughed her hearty, lovely laugh, "Patrick would love to meet you, won't he James?" Even though she had lived in Devon for some years, she still pronounced it "Patreek" and I loved her for it. She made the word sound like a colour or a fragrance, and without waiting for a response from James who anyway sat mutely, she glanced at the clock on the mantelpiece and said "He'll be home from school soon," and pouring brown thick tea into a cup, repeated with a chuckle "Patrick would love to meet you."

XXVII

A few days after the scalpel incident, the police arrived at our house and arrested Kary. She was in the bath at the time and left, still wet, wearing the first clothes she could find (the dirty ones she had just taken off) and, of course, handcuffs. At first, we thought she might have been arrested for stealing hospital equipment, that the authorities had counted, tracked back and concluded correctly. We thought it a little harsh if this was the case. Angelo was instantly thrown into frantic mode, anxiously questioning the two police officers who studiously ignored him and levelled their comments at a far less vigorous me: "A serious allegation has been made. We'll be taking her to the police station in town. I suggest you give it some time and come down there to speak to the desk sergeant." The vision of Kary being led down the road to the police car is still fresh in my mind – her reluctant stumpy legs, her expression a mix of mild panic and despair, she looked like an overgrown school kid being forced to go to school against her will.

It took a while to calm Angelo who eventually accepted that if she had been arrested for the "serious allegation" of stealing the scalpel, they wouldn't keep her for long. It would be a slap on the wrist, an hour in a cell and then home. So it was, in fact, the calming of Angelo that prompted a revelation and led us to discover the real reason why Kary had been arrested.

Angelo is a doer. I knew him well enough to know that in times of panic, words are not as effective as deeds, so I suggested that we checked Kary's room, ostensibly to find the scalpel, but also to pacify Angelo's kinaesthetic needs. Her room was a shambolic jumble of clothes, books, magazines, make-up and snacks – some half eaten. It was more untidy than usual, I imagined because she hadn't had the time to scoop up the usual debris. She had obviously been snacking on crisps and some crunched under foot as we entered her room. Angelo opened the curtains and pinkish morning light strobed in through the trees outside making the room look like something from an old movie – a set-up scene, contrived in its untidiness. It was hard to know where to begin. Knowing Kary as we did, if she still had the scalpel, it could be anywhere. Given that I had left it on her bed a few days before, and even though there was no reason to suggest it would still be there, it seemed perfectly logical for me at the time to straighten her shabby duvet into some sort of order, hopeful that the scalpel would fall the floor. Dust particles rose ineffectually from the bed and quickly plunged back down to safety as I flapped the duvet a couple of times to release anything interesting. A smell of oniony body odour instantly pervaded the air prompting Angelo to open a sticky window for the stale air to escape through. "Nothing here," I said, to bridge some sort of communication. Glancing round the room, Kary's life in a nutshell, I noticed items I hadn't known she owned:

a collection of shells, some of them broken had been left on her bedside table – these must have been several years old, we hadn't been to the sea since we were teenagers; a half-full bottle of French perfume, upturned, on her dressing table, probably a present from Clive; in amongst the rest of the rubbish on the floor was a cardboard box with the words "Turbo Hairdryer and Straighteners" in bold writing on the side, ironic in the fact that the box remained unopened and comical at the thought of Kary's hair being "turboed" in any way. A Polaroid photograph of Clive had been wonkily placed in a too-big wooden frame on the window sill, his face, faded now and pale and fixed in a false smile for the camera.

It was Angelo who suggested we look a little closer, and in unison we both rifled through drawers and boxes. In amongst the chaos of empty containers and used make-up, the sadness of her life was so starkly shown: disposable items were not disposed of, they were kept, collected without any order, not let go of, symptomatic of her general life philosophy. Sticky wrappers, presumably mementoes of unfaithful meetings in coffee shops, that once contained sugar or sweetener littered her bedside drawer and stuck accusingly to my hands as I rummaged though. There was a business card with an unfamiliar telephone number scribbled on the back, a picture of a satellite dish on the front had been coloured in with blue biro and hearts drawn childishly on each bent and scrunched corner. A shorthand notebook, its wire spiral contorted by age, contained shopping lists with crossings out and childish drawings of faces, houses and flowers. The minutia of Kary's existence was here and we, Angelo and I, were ransacking it. Then we found it. We found the scalpel. It was in what Kary called her "secret drawer" – not secret at all as they usually aren't. It was wrapped in paper, white A4, printed with invasive black ink. On the face of it, not written by Kary, printed from elsewhere, maybe the internet. Reading what was printed on the sheets, I was instantly taken back to a conversation Kary had wanted to have with me some time before, a conversation which had seemed so meaningless at the time, yet now I knew this was why Kary had been arrested. This was what we had been looking for. The piece was headed *"Foetal Abduction, the facts"*. Together, Angelo and I read each line and a dreadful possibility dawned ever more clearly. Re-wrapping the scalpel in the heavy paper, I shoved it deep into my handbag.

Police stations are less welcoming than they should be. Don't be fooled by automatic doors or the blast of dry heat from above, or the fact that the old fluorescent lighting has been replaced by trendy down-lighters. Pay attention to the expression on the desk sergeant's face as you advance towards him; don't overlook the queasy smell of crime, and that heat? It's meant to make you sweat along with the rest of them. This was our first experience of law enforcement and I clung onto Angelo's smooth hand, glad that he was there, feeling a twanging, churning guilt about something I hadn't done.

The desk sergeant appraised us wordlessly at first, I wondered momentarily if they trained police officers to cultivate that look. We must have taken just a moment too long to break the silence because, blinking in that has-he-fallen-asleep kind of way that some people can perform, the desk sergeant asked, rather unconvincingly if he could help us in any way. I explained why we were there, noticing his expressing change to weary anticipation as he asked us to "take a seat" and then disappearing through a heavy security locked door. Posters on the wall advised and instructed us not to put up with domestic violence, to "shop a criminal", to join a neighbourhood watch. Cartoon images of the perfect and the immoral, the victim and the criminal were all about us. Sitting there, with only the hum of heat and Angelo for company, I wondered which category we fell into, the angel or the devil. Sooner than I expected, the desk sergeant re-appeared, and behind him a man who beckoned us through into another room.

"Interview room 2" it said on the door and I hesitated for a second before entering, aware that the handbag I was carrying contained some fairly damning evidence. Wasn't there a rule about police interviews? Shouldn't we have been cautioned or offered a solicitor? What about that phone call that everyone on tv was allowed to make? My defensive hackles must have been visibly rising because as if reading my mind, the officer, by now in the room and about to sit down gave a little laugh and said "Oh, don't worry, I'm not interviewing you, I just thought we needed some privacy." I was relieved. Privacy was fine. Motioning to the two chairs opposite him, the man sat down and we entered. The room was a small one, cramped and claustrophobic because of lack of windows or air. Once the door closed, it seemed like a contained cell lit by a long fluorescent light. A medium sized old wooden table which could have doubled as a dining table was placed centrally against the far wall, chunks of plaster missing from the wall implied the table was frequently moved with force an inch or so either way. Damaged red vinyl padded the chairs and a puff of air escaped from the tears as we sat down. A tape recorder sat, unplugged, on the floor. I felt as if I was in tv police drama and suppressed a sudden urge to refer to the man as "Guv". The man looked at us both in turn. It was difficult to pin down how old he might be. Obviously past the age where lighting didn't matter, his face was lined around the forehead and darkish rings circled his eyes. His hair, though thinning on top a little, was chocolate brown and styled in that careless, rumpled way favoured by young football fans – one of the lads no doubt. As a "plain clothed" police officer, there was nothing plain about his choice of clothes: designer jacket, beautifully cut, and purple shirt, open casually at the neck revealing a clutch of thick chest hair sprouting high up. He could have been twenty five or forty five, I really couldn't work it out. His face was animated and his voice heavy with the local accent as he reached into his silk jacket pocket to produce his ID. "DC Jones" he announced, flipping open the black wallet revealing a less than complimentary photograph. Angelo and I nodded as if we understood, heartened by DC Jones' affability.

"I'm glad you've come," he started, averting his eyes in the way that people do when they're trying to organise a set of complex thoughts into words. "We've arrested Kary, but we haven't charged her yet." The word "yet" was emphasised as he made eye contact with each of us in turn. Angelo and I remained mute. DC Jones continued, leaning forward and clasping his hands together on the table exposing the backs of two hairy hands with perfectly manicured nails and a large clunky gold wristwatch which was probably designer. "We received a very serious allegation from a Mr. Pratt?" I cringed a little at his choice of intonation. The high rising tone of the young or uneducated had irritated me from the moment it had become fashionable to use and I refused to succumb to the inevitable fillers of "yes" or "mm" that such a poor linguistic technique underhandedly requested of the listener. Of course I knew who Mr. Pratt was, in fact I'd always felt sorry for Clive having a surname with such obvious connotations, but if DC Jones wanted me to say, he needed to ask, not hint. After a pause in which I was steadfastly unwilling to respond DC Jones leaned forward a little more and continued "It seems that Kary went round to Mr. Pratt's house and threatened Mrs. Pratt with what looked to be a sharp implement of some kind." The way the light was falling from above darkened the shadows of growth on DC Jones' upper lip and chin making him look quite handsome, and nearer to twenty five now. "Mrs. Pratt is quite heavily pregnant and the allegation is that Kary pushed her to the floor, threatening to perform a caesarean section on her?" There it was again, an unnecessary use of the questioning intonation. I began to wonder at DC Jones' intellectual capacity. "Fortunately, Mr. Pratt arrived home from work just in time, disturbing what could have been a very serious incident indeed. Kary scarpered though and, of course Mr. Pratt was most concerned with the welfare of his wife to give chase." DC Jones leaned back in his chair and the dark circles under his eyes re-appeared with the differing light. "Mrs. Pratt and her baby are fine, thank God, but this is a very serious allegation against Kary." For not using the high rising tone, I rewarded him with a nod. None of what I had heard surprised me, except perhaps the fact that Kary had been unsuccessful in her attempt at foetal abduction. Her timing had always been out – an hour earlier and she might have pulled it off. I shuffled in my seat, my thighs beginning to stick uncomfortably to the vinyl and kicked my handbag so that it skittered a little under the table. Instant guilt made me apologise – what for I wasn't sure, but whatever it was jolted my thinking and, partly in an effort to distract my own thoughts from the scalpel in my handbag, partly because I knew Kary so very well, I said "Is he sure it was Kary?" This noticeably threw DC Jones who blinked a couple of times in quick succession and said "What do you mean?" A plot, a defence really was forming in my mind and I hoped Angelo would just stay quiet. "Well, is Mr. Pratt sure it was Kary?" DC Jones thought for a second, averting his eyes again and I noticed how large his nose was, just a little too large to make him traditionally handsome. "He seems sure." He said slowly, "In fact, he's been very open with us. I understand that he and Kary know each other quite well." I knew the euphemism was designed to encourage me to confirm what Clive had said, to spill the beans about Clive's affair with Kary but if my suspicions were correct, we could still get Kary off the hook. I waited for a moment before saying "Kary is a very private person DC Jones, I suspect she has said very little to you." And it was at this moment that I knew I was on to a winner. DC Jones looked straight at me and at first I thought I might have got it wrong, then he sighed heavily, running his hairy hand through his designer hair style. "Look," he said eventually, "I'll be straight with you. Mr. Pratt has given us chapter and verse on the history and is absolutely sure it was Kary he saw her tear-arsing out of his kitchen. Mrs. Pratt, well, she's in shock really but the vague description she's given seems to be Kary. I mean, she is, well, distinctive in looks isn't she? But Kary, well," he sighed again, "she won't cough. She's said nothing. Nothing at all."

Just as I had thought.

And here followed a pack of lies, based, as they usually are in some version of the truth, about how we were aware that Kary and Clive had been an item for a while but it was over now (true), how Kary had moved on (here's where it gets a bit fuzzy), in fact, she had been in a new relationship but had recently and sadly lost a baby of her own and that it was in fact Mr. Pratt who seemed to want to rekindle their relationship. I explained how he had recently visited our house to see Kary (basically true) and had ended up taking her to hospital (true), I added that, in my opinion, Mr. Pratt was still keen on Kary and that not only was he a proven liar – lying to his wife by conducting an affair with Kary, but that he had become almost obsessively jealous when he realised Kary was pregnant by someone else, that he couldn't bear the thought that she had moved on with her life, and that all this was a shameful attempt to discredit her and make himself look like a hero. Furthermore, I told DC Jones that he and his colleagues were welcome to come to our house to search it for clues but that I was 100% certain that they would find nothing to implicate Kary in this terrible crime and that in my opinion, they should be out there trying to find the real culprit, if indeed there was one to find.

I couldn't have been prouder of myself. It was a fantastic performance.

As I spoke DC Jones looked at me with utter incredulity, shaking his head slowly from side to side. Then a wry, rather creepy smile stretched his mouth and, folding his undoubtedly hairy arms, he asked "What exactly *is* your relationship with Kary?"

XXVIII

Relationships were something I had never questioned before. I knew I was having a "special" relationship with Angelo, but I just didn't think about relationships until my conversation with James. I suppose, obtusely, most fifteen year olds don't overtly think about arrangements with people with whom they are having a really close relationship and I was no exception, being totally immersed in an understanding with Kary, Angelo as well as the Doctor added new meaning to not being able to see the wood for the trees. So sitting in James' living room, waiting for Patrick to arrive from school was more than just mind-boggling. Here I was with a whole new set of relationships to deal with and, of course, the child inside me created yet more – it would be the grandchild of James and Dawn. Sitting waiting for Patrick I tried to drink tea, finding it increasingly difficult as nerves constricted my throat and gnarled up my stomach. Nerves made me aware of my every bodily function: muscles contracting and relaxing, sinews straining and juices flowing, and as I sat, ever more tense, I was astounded at my own stupidity. Why had I never asked any questions? My life was clearly not normal. James' life was normal: wife, child, home.

Patrick would be the one I would need to speak to, after all he was having the life I should have had. Lost in self absorbtion, I didn't notice that Dawn and James were watching me from the other side of the room and it was only when Dawn spoke to me directly that I snapped out of myself.

"How are you?" She ventured. Her voice was kind, a deep throaty voice as dark and smooth as her skin, but her question shocked me and I blinked stupidly, unused to such genuine concern. I could have given a placatory answer, but heard myself say "I don't know."

Dawn's face settled into a crumple of interest and she moved forward in the tatty armchair. Not taking her chocolate brown eyes off me for a second, she said quietly, "You don't know?"

My silence answered her question.

"Who's looking after you?" Another question I couldn't answer.

"Have you seen a doctor or a midwife?"

Now, this one, I thought I could answer. Of course I had seen the Doctor and I started explaining to Dawn my understanding of how I had come to be in Devon. And as I heard my childish voice recounting events, it all seemed so suddenly bizarre, so strange and abnormal, that the look on her face – a mix of astonishment, sorrow and disbelief seemed to me to be so totally appropriate. Then something peculiar happened: Dawn rose from her seat – the woman I still believed could be my mother – she rose from her seat, dipped down to her knees in front of me and curled her hot arms around me in an embrace so tight I thought I could happily suffocate in the love it signified. Her curly hair was remarkably soft against my cheek and she carried with her a warm buttery smell that I couldn't quite place. It was easy to hug her back. She seemed to hold me for a long time and her grip didn't loosen so that when she eventually let me go, the feel the pressure on my flesh remained. I don't think she would have stopped holding me if it hadn't been for the sound of a throbbing engine outside the house, unmistakeably a bus.

Both James and Dawn stood up simultaneously and looked out of their window, which vibrated intermittently, a scientific reaction to the arrival of the bus.

"It's Patrick." James said by way of explanation and then both he and Dawn left the room to disappear down the hallway.

I heard the front door open and felt a gush of damp air rush in. The stark change in temperature made me shiver, jolting me back to a reality I thought I knew. Adrenaline was pumping inside me though and I straightened up, wondering whether it would be best to meet the person I had already decided was my brother standing up or sitting down. Voices were retreating and then advancing and I could feel that sense of imminence in which fear mixes with paralysis, so despite the confusion of excitement, you know the moment will be clearly etched in your memory forever. Heart beating fast and loud, I decided to stand up and in so doing, knocked the nearby bookshelf with its children's picture books and a book fell to the floor. Quickly, I picked it up, aware that excessive noisy movement in the hallway was about to herald Patrick's arrival. As the front door closed with that loose fitting sound old doors have, I fumbled with the book in my hand, a small well-thumbed little book called "Birthday" and on the front cover a picture of a boy blowing out candles on an impossibly brightly coloured cake. Quickly, I slotted it back onto the shelf, smoothed my unruly, unwashed hair in an effort to look vaguely respectable and tried to look friendly, but suspect I just looked hopeful and a little pathetic.

I should have known. I should have guessed by the commotion in the hall. Those unusual sounds, the tones of voices, the bumps and knocks, for pity's sake the books on the shelf should had been a big hint. Looking back now, I could have worked it out if I had tried, the clues were clear. I might not have come up with an accurate conclusion, after all James and Dawn had been so friendly and forthcoming – not that that makes any difference, but I could have been in the ball-park as the Americans say. What I couldn't have anticipated was my own reaction, and my own inability to mask it.

XXIX

My performance in front of DC Jones was nothing less than Oscar winning but its success relied upon Kary's continuing silence. My handbag seemed heavy yet there was only my almost-empty purse and the hastily wrapped scalpel in it. I had challenged DC Jones to search our house for a weapon and said I resented him asking personal questions of me when he should surely stick to the facts. I was completely in role as the affronted semi-accused. I revelled in the fact that every now and then his brown designer shoes gently skimmed my handbag on the floor. I thought it hilarious that he was so close to the truth yet too apparently stupid to know, and it added to my feeling of confidence and superiority. I finished my performance with a flourish.

"DC Jones," I commanded, "I'm surprised you don't arrest me and Angelo here. Maybe you think we're in on it. In fact," and here I reached down, grabbed my handbag in audacious disbelief, "why don't you search my bag to check for sharp implements?"

I slammed my handbag down on the table and made challenging, silent eye contact with the now slightly apprehensive police officer. Never for a second was he interested in that bag and he shoved it back to me with a sort of apologetic expression used only by so-called "professionals" who feel they have justifiably been backed into a corner and fear that the litigious society in which we live might turn on its head a little more and give credence to any complaint against them.

No more needed to be said and I grabbed my bag and stood up in confirmation that the conversation, indeed the subject, was closed, closely followed by Angelo and DC Jones.

We took Kary straight home. She was, of course, a mess and retreated immediately to her room, lumbering up the stairs without a word.

I had noticed that Angelo was unusually quiet – that sort of quiet that could be a prelude to an argument with other people, but which, for Angelo was a sign that he was concentrating or upset, or both. I knew how to handle it and as he sat quietly down on the sofa in our living room, I scrooched close to him, pushing my arm through his and nuzzling his lovely neck. "What is it?" I whispered close to his ear, tracing the contours of his jaw-line with my other hand. I knew he wouldn't respond immediately, so continued nuzzling before turning his face to mine so that I could feel his breath on my face and his lips were too close not to kiss. But I didn't kiss them, I asked again, "Angelo, what is it? Tell me." Without taking his eyes off mine, without changing his neutral expression, Angelo said, as if it explained everything, "You lied. You lied to the police officer."

Such an obvious observation, so simplistic in its communication threw me instantly and I was immediately on the defense.

"Yes." I agreed, standing up and trying to stay patient but failing, "Because if I had told the truth Angelo, Kary would have been arrested and thrown into prison for attempted murder or attempted baby snatching or whatever was going on in her mind."

"I know," Angelo said calmly, still seated, "but you could have told the truth."

Patience now completely evaporated, I strutted about the living room, as angry as he was calm, with a total mental block on his thinking, concerned only with what I considered to be unnecessary criticism of me - the saviour - or Kary. I simply couldn't believe it, and my reaction snowballed as I reminded him of what DC Jones had told us, of why Kary had been arrested, reminded him about the scalpel, of how we had searched Kary's room, of how she was unstable after the miscarriage. I thought I had done the only thing possible to save Kary. To foist the blame onto Clive was the only way I could do it at the time. In reality, of course, I felt a bitter-sweet pleasure in being presented with a perfect opportunity to punish Clive for what he had done to both Kary and Jane. By the time I had finished, I was hot with indignity, tearful that my good deed had been questioned. Angelo, affected by my outburst, stood up before I had finished speaking and held me to him until I had quietened, tapping my back with his slender fingers as if I was a baby in need of comfort, not a grown woman who had just been solely responsible for the release of a poor unfortunate but none-the-less guilty Kary. When he thought I was listening, Angelo kissed my head and said quietly "You could have just told the truth. The things we know about Kary, we know by accident or by snooping. We don't actually know anything. You didn't need to lie to cover up for her. The truth would have covered it all up, wouldn't it?"

Standing there, leaning against his chest, listening to the steady beat of his honest heart and feeling the cold dampness of my tears grow against his tee-shirt, I knew he was right. It really would have taken some proof that Kary had committed this crime – Jane didn't know her and may not have been to identify her, Clive only caught a glimpse of someone running from his house in the dark, he was only surmising it was Kary. Angelo was absolutely right, if I had just told the truth, that we knew nothing, the odds were that Kary would have been sent home through lack of evidence. I felt a fool and vowed never to lie again. And it was Angelo gently pointing out my mistake, his uncontaminated thinking that made me realise that lying was something I had been involved with for too long.

We kissed for a long time with at least part of me hoping that some of Angelo's goodness would rub off or transfer to me in the process, and so much was I hypnotised by this idea that I didn't notice Kary's arrival in the room until she was sitting down in the spot where Angelo and I had been. She was the first to speak.

"You've been in my room." She said, her monotone voice giving no clue as to how she felt about such an invasion but her face running through a range of expressions in an effort, I presumed, to find the right one.

"Yes," I said, honestly, glancing at Angelo for confirmation, "we were worried when the police came and we knew about the…you know."

Kary hesitated only for a second before articulating clearly "You had no right to go into my room."

Here Angelo took over, "We were worried about you Kary. Everything we have done is because we wanted to get you out of trouble. We know you've been through a difficult time."

No lies there.

Kary rose slowly to her feet, looking directly up at Angelo, her eyes fixing him with a lacerating glare. For a moment I expected her to attack one or both of us, but she stood steadily in front of us, directing her comments to Angelo, speaking with that robotic clarity saved usually for the old, deaf or foreign, "You should have left me there. I did it. I went to Clive's house. I had a plan. I wanted his baby. You should have left me to rot in that police cell. Anything would be better than this."

She spat final words through clenched, uneven teeth but didn't move any closer to us. I noticed with apprehension my handbag on the floor near her foot and tried to cut any telepathic links to her which might make her question where we might have hidden the scalpel. Truthfully, I felt for the first time in fear of my life. Kary's grim demeanour could only be bad news. But none of us moved, and if it hadn't been for the tinny sound of a car engine parking with dangerous, clumsy swiftness outside our house, I'm not sure how the spell would have been broken. All eyes outside now, we watched in silence as Clive leapt out of his car, slamming the door with such force that the whole car creaked and rocked for a while afterwards. He sprinted to our door, battering and shouting like a lunatic. Still we all stood, rooted to the spot, with only our facial expressions revealing fear or anticipation. We all knew that we were thinking the same thing: that if Clive entered our house, he was so angry, something terrible could happen. Clive continued banging on our door, maybe what we were hearing was kicking as well and I knew, despite what Angelo had said about not needing to lie, what I had to do. As I advanced down the hallway, my handbag tucked under my arm, those patterns, those loose tiles seemed somehow emphasised by the evening light falling in from the glass above the front door. Clive seemed to be shouting obscenities, but I couldn't hear exactly what. Grabbing the ancient door handle, I twisted it and opened the door. Clive was puce with fury. He was wearing jeans that looked too big around the waist and too short in the leg, his shirt was buttoned oddly and he needed a shave. When he saw it was me, he faltered a little and, taking my opportunity, I said evenly "Come in Clive". He stepped into the house and said with measured calm "Where is she?" and I motioned up the hallway to the living room, watching his lollopy gait trudge with great forcefulness up and right in through the open living room door. My hand was still on the door lock and when I opened the door I could see his car parked on the skew in the road. Voices wafted down the hallway and I knew I needed to act quickly. The air outside was prickly cold, I predicted a frost overnight, and as I got into Clive's car, left unlocked in his haste to get to Kary, I noticed inside was not much warmer – I suspected the heater was as faulty as the rest of it. The glove compartment wasn't locked and was full of bits of paper, MOTs, bills, tissues and so forth. I reached into my handbag, took out the scalpel, carefully wiped it clean with the sleeve of my tee-shirt and placed it in the glove compartment of Clive's Ford Fiesta. Snapping the compartment shut I found myself disagreeing with Angelo's assertion that there was no need to lie.

At that moment I needed to lie.

XXX

An empty wheelchair, black with silver wheels stuck with clumsily placed brightly coloured stickers saying "Well Done!" and "I'm a genius!" clattered into the room. Pushing it with no apparent fear or anticipation as to my presence was a boy whose age was impossible to guess. His fat hands clasped the rubber at the rear of the chair, virtually non existent fingernails lined the tips of stubby fingers. A very large green sweatshirt emphasised his lumpy, overweight look. There was an emblem of some kind just below his left shoulder, probably the name of a school but I couldn't see in the fast dimming light and anyway wasn't driven to read it because I was far more interested in his face. Light brown skin stretched across a face that was wider than it was long. A disproportionately small pug nose was a feature that was completely overwhelmed by eyes that seemed exaggeratedly slanted upwards and outwards across his face. A broad, open mouth revealed a big dry tongue which, as he stood studying me with interest, moved in spasms back and forth as if trying to dampen itself.

"This is Patrick," Dawn said, edging her way into the room whilst at the same time grabbing Patrick's elbow and steering him and the wheelchair towards me. Patrick moved uncertainly, knuckles white as he held on to the wheelchair, feet moving flatly along the carpeted floor.

"Say 'Hello' Patrick," Dawn said encouragingly, still holding onto his arm whilst deftly steering the wheelchair away from him and folding flat it in one smooth motion. Patrick hesitated for a second, his hands still fixed in position, holding onto something, then, realising there was nothing there, lowering his arms and sniffing loudly.

"Say 'Hello' Patrick," Dawn persisted gently, and he looked round at her, searching her face for something, his profile a jutting jaw-line and the back of his head almost completely flat giving him a bulldoggish look. Dawn raised her eyebrows at him and nodded slowly and he turned to face me again. His crinkly black hair glistened with an artificial quality, almost as if it was wet and his narrow toffee brown eyes gazed in my general direction. That purple tongue throbbed enthusiastically and a droplet of white saliva escaped from the corner of his mouth, dripping down his shallow chin and onto his sweatshirt leaving a silvery trail.

"Hello Patrick," his voice was muffled by his obstructive tongue and flatly monotone in its delivery. His face broke into a wide smile at the sound of his own joke. Stretched skin on his cheeks changed colour from coffee red to silver brown, his mouth took on the shape of a half moon and his slitty eyes closed almost completely with glee. Releasing an explosive nasal guffaw, more saliva escaped from the corners of his mouth and as Dawn dabbed it away with a brisk, maternal efficiency, some escaped from the ball of pink tissue paper and dribbled onto her fingers and she wiped it on her skirt with such matter-of-factness, without embarrassment that I knew she expected nothing less from anyone else, including me. I knew she just expected everyone else to simply be able to wipe away the idea that Patrick's difference was anything other than acceptable.

Truth was, I had never seen anyone or anything so ugly in my life.

James, standing behind them both, caught my eye and I could see a look on his face that registered my own. Oblivious to all this, Dawn soldiered on:

"Shake hands nicely now," and, holding his hand, she raised his arm to waist level and I watched as his floppy fingers came to life in front of him in a ritual I could see he had gone through many times before. But the thought of touching him, of having his skin on mine repulsed me to the point of sickness and I am uncertain, even to this day, of what I would have done if James hadn't stepped forward and said "Oh now, come on Patrick old boy, let's get you washed up before dinner eh? Can't be shaking hands when you haven't washed them can we?" and he led the benign Patrick, his hand still freakishly held out in front of him in mock hand-shake, out of the room.

Both Dawn and I watched the two of them disappear, she lovingly, me with a growing feeling of revulsion that must have been written on my face. Dawn turned to me and I could see her quickly assessing my reaction – surely, I thought, something she must have been used to. Still looking at me, she sat down, and I did the same, inept and unable to say anything. I thought she might comment on the look on my face and tried to change my expression but was aware that no real change was taking place. I couldn't think of anything to say and wished Dawn would speak.

Instead she continued to gaze directly at me, her face a mask of calm and patience. She completed a picture of acceptance and serenity: her smooth brown hands clasped in her lap; her workish clothes beginning to look tatty; the chair in which she sat grubby and worn and the folded wheelchair which leant awkwardly against it; the picture books on the shelf, wordless and immature. All of this seemed to me to be a picture of such depressing happiness that I was afraid I would be sucked into it, unable ever to emerge. Already a sense of entrapment was washing over me. If James and Dawn were my parents, then Patrick was my brother. Patrick, with his vague, retarded stare and his malformed body and face. If it hadn't been for the possible link between us, I would have felt compassion, even affection, but it was the possibility that we could be siblings that I found revolting that changed everything. Patrick was imperfect in a way I had never really considered anyone could be and I was surprising myself with the strength of my own reaction. Suddenly, and in an effort to abate the inevitable self-loathing which would occur when I reflected on my thoughts later, I decided that he could not be my brother. Dawn could not be my mother. Her skin was black and her features were broad and large, unlike mine. I must have been stupid, I thought, to even consider it. Looking back now, I see my own egocentrism as pernicious and stupid but it was precisely that, my own obsession with myself, which is key to the events which followed, and, it could be argued, which had been key to events which preceded.

Dawn broke the thick silence between us. "Are you staying for tea?" and I could barely answer "no thank you" quickly enough, adding I had only really come to collect the mobile phone charger. Dawn nodded in some sort of understanding and then, following another silence, asked me if I had any doctor's appointments organised. I shook my head. "Well, you really should you know." She sounded like my mother even if she wasn't. And then she said something that jolted me into reality. "If I had been checked more regularly, maybe we would have been more prepared for Patrick."

I blinked at her, amazed that she had broached the subject with such bluntness.

"What do you mean?" I asked, not wanting this line of conversation to lapse just yet.

"Well," here Dawn began to look the most uncomfortable I had seen her so far, "I just thought everything would be ok – you do don't you?" She looked at me hopefully, "And I just didn't manage to attend my appointments so I missed all the scan appointments, and missed the time when I could have had an amniocentesis test. We just had no idea that Patrick would be Down's Syndrome, and if I had had the tests, I would have been, well, more prepared."

A wave of sympathy mixed with a now all too familiar self-loathing consumed me. I hated myself for feeling anything other than concern for all of them. But only for a moment. The possible link to James, Dawn and Patrick burned through. The question rose in my throat and I had to ask it.

"What would you have done Dawn, if you'd known?"

Her answer seemed to come from far away – a stock answer probably, one that had been given many times before and would be given many times still. I don't know exactly what she said because my own thoughts interrupted, shoving my mind into a turmoil, making links and connections to areas I hadn't considered, or thought I could consider.

Egocentricity made me ignorant to her answer and made me focus on what I was going to do with the child inside me.

XXXI

Waking up next to Angelo is always such a wonderful experience. At night, I must just attach myself unconsciously to him, wrapping my limbs and muscles and body around him, inhaling the muskiness of his skin, yearning for confirmation of his presence. That morning was no exception.

I awoke early and because it was a Sunday I knew he didn't have to work, I snuggled closer to him and he replied by tracing the outline of my shoulder and arm with his fingertip. My skin warmed to his touch and that prickly sensation was replaced with an ardent need to kiss him. Early morning light filtered purple through the curtains and made the room feel somehow exotic, foreign almost. Outside was quiet. Angelo's lips were hot and wet and the skin on his face smelt sharp and lemony. Night time beard growth peppered his chin and I ran my hand along his jaw line, feeling the stubble catch every now and then. Angelo skimmed the back of his hand across my face and through my hair, tingling the roots and sending spasms of relaxed joy right through me.

Angelo and I.

We had always been so happy with each other, really I suppose we had always loved each other. And as we lay together that morning, only one thing would spoil our happiness. Only one thing had the power or knowledge of how to interrupt, to intervene, to intrude: Kary.

At first we ignored her, both of us as content and relaxed as we could be, given that we knew Kary had begun patrolling up and down outside our bedroom door, muttering something incomprehensible. Her voice and her footsteps advanced and receded, advanced and receded until neither Angelo or I could bare it any longer. This was Kary's code. She would not enter our room, but she would make us feel a horrible discomfort. Angelo released himself from me and his retreating body left mine cool and wanting. Slipping his arms hastily through the baggy sleeves of my bathrobe, oblivious to looking ridiculous, Angelo opened the door and Kary stood, hands on her hips, waiting on the landing. She knew it wouldn't take much to elicit a response from us.

Kary had not entered our bedroom since we had been teenagers and she stood, disabled too much by morals or ritual to cross the threshold. In her hand she held a newspaper, rolled up in the way that newspaper delivery people do. Sitting up in bed I could see the familiar emblem of the local newspaper, red and green in the corner under Kary's fingers. We received this dire example of a tabloid each week. It usually took a couple of minutes to scan and throw out. It was not so much full of news as advertisements. Local tradesmen advertised extensively in it, but the classified section could be quite amusing I always thought: the lonely hearts with their secret acronyms and peculiar needs, the "sales and wants" where people tried to offload junk they didn't want and buy junk they didn't need and the births, marriages and deaths filled with dour badly written ditties penned by the drunk, the stupid and the distressed. At first I thought the newspaper's roving reporter might have picked up on the story about an intruder at Clive's house and half imagined the headline "Scalpel Stalker gives Cops the Slip". Kary would be mad about that alright, but it was difficult to work out what was on her mind as she stood there outside our bedroom door. It could have been anger or agitation, but it seemed to fall somewhere between madness and incredulity.

"Anything wrong Kary?" Angelo was wise to employ tact at moments like this, any doubt as to Kary's mood was enough to make us exercise control.

Kary unfurled the newspaper in one fail swoop like a medieval messenger dressed in floral polyester. From my vantage point, it looked like a page of classified advertisements and I could vaguely make out some black and white photographs amidst the columns of text. Kary said nothing but pointed with a stubby finger at a few lines about half way down the page. Angelo took the newspaper from her, turning towards the light slightly to read the small letters and his lips moved, gently, silently mouthing the words he read. The realisation on his face was swift and, glancing quickly at me, he reverted his attention to Kary and embraced her, patting her shoulders whilst rocking slowly from side to side. The newspaper was still in his hands and it swung limply from side to side between his fingertips. I knew it would be useless to ask questions at that point so sat still in bed, clutching the duvet to my chest, waiting for Angelo to stop holding her, knowing that any movement from me could destroy the moment. Sure enough, after a couple of seconds, Kary peeled herself off Angelo and stood, dejected, head slumped. Angelo said something to her which I couldn't make out and she nodded obediently before skulking away and downstairs. Angelo watched her go, then returned to the room and closed the door, the newspaper still in his hand.

"What?" I asked excitedly.

Angelo handed me the newspaper, pointing wordlessly in the same way that Kary had to a fading announcement which read "PRATT. To Clive and Jane, a baby girl, Carrie, a beautiful sister for Harry."

It was easy to imagine how Kary must be feeling and I looked at Angelo, shaking my head, astonished at the level of insensitivity that Clive had shown yet at the same time interested in his motives for such strange decisions. True, some parents do try to synchronise their offspring's names so that some form of poetic device is used – assonance, alliteration or rhyme being favourite ways of successfully pissing off siblings, and I was sure both Harry and Carrie would indeed be very pissed off in the fullness of time. However, surely the mere *sound* of the noun was just too tactless, too *close* to "Kary"? And why *announce* it? What did he hope to achieve?

Angelo and I swiftly dressed and for more than a few moments I felt real pangs of annoyance that my Sunday morning with Angelo had been destroyed by what must be at least in part bitterness on Clive's part and the usual neediness of Kary.

Kary was in the kitchen. She had made three mugs of tea and had put them on the table, signifying where we should all sit: Kary

Me Angelo

Angelo and I held hands under the table and Kary cradled her mug of tea in her two hands. Angelo put the newspaper on the table. No one spoke. We all drank our tea in silence, me trying to avoid constricting my throat muscles so much that that irritating squeaky gulp produced by the very nervous or the very rude did not happen, until it must have occurred to each of us that one of us needed to speak, to say something. Angelo maintained a downward gaze, not looking at the newspaper or the mug of tea. Kary's glassy stare seemed to be entirely inward. I began to feel the adverse effects of the silence which was starting to choke me into squeaky gulp territory.

"Well Kary," I heard myself say, "I think this announcement is just a typical example of Clive's utter devotion towards you."

Kary squinted at me, tilting her head as if she didn't quite understand me but wanting me to continue.

"I mean," I said in low tones, leaning across and picking up the newspaper, "this is typical of Clive. I can just imagine his pathetic thinking." Actually I could imagine nothing of the kind but my rambling nonsense had at least cracked open the strangling silence and sounded completely supportive.

"Think of it this way: Clive is so...obsessed with you Kary, that when his wife gives birth to their daughter, their "beautiful" daughter, he has to name her after you, and then, not content with that, he has to announce it to the world, *knowing* that you will read it, *knowing* that you will interpret it in the wrong way – thinking he was simply being tactless, but all the time, he's secretly hoping, in that…pathetic way of his, that deep down, you'll know that he loved you but realise that he's trapped now with two children, chained to Jane, and the only way he can be with you is through his own daughter."

Amazed at my own claptrap, I stopped talking, flabbergasted at my own inventiveness, a total confirmation of the illusion of group productivity. What I had said did, in fact, demonstrate the total opposite to what I actually thought, and I knew without him saying that Angelo would agree with me. Clive, in my opinion, couldn't care less about Kary. She had been his "bit of rough", his bit on the side. She had been a willing partner, the change that was as good as the rest, but only temporarily. In my opinion, she had meant nothing to him and this announcement confirmed it. It rubbed her nose in the fact that she was apparently unable to have children. It reminded her of her misspelt name, it corrected her almost. It reduced her, symbolically at least, not just to a child but to a baby and it reminded her of her ugliness against the baby's beauty and innocence. Because of the lack of detail you might usually expect in such joyful advertisements such as the weight of the child, when and where it was born, there was, in my opinion, an antiseptic quality to the announcement of the arrival of Baby Carrie which aimed to expunge Clive of any guilt which, rightfully, he should feel forever. No flowery adjectives here, no delighted adverbs to mask the fact that Clive and Jane were together. The end.

Kary, of course, subscribed immediately to my sycophancy. Naturally she believed that Clive was totally infatuated with her and this announcement in this two bit tabloid was a coded message to her which, far from merely announcing the birth of a child, was, in fact, announcing his undying, everlasting love.

I shook my head as Kary revelled in the prospect of being loved from afar by the limp and lily-livered, and aptly named, Clive Pratt. At least the tension was broken now and in the back of my mind there still burned a desire for Angelo which might not be able to wait for evening.

"Do you know what you need?" I said, mustering excitement mostly for myself. Kary shook her head, her eyes wide.

"Shopping therapy." I said.

Kary frowned.

"Oh, now come on Kary," I could afford to be daring, I had her on side now, "Sunday trading was designed for days like this. You should go into town and treat yourself to some new outfits and make up – you deserve it, you've had a hard time recently."

Angelo squeezed my hand under the table, probably pleased with my obvious plan to get her out of the house. I waited. But not for long. A wide grin spread across Kary's face.

"You're right." She said, standing up and making for the door, "See you later."

Successes, even minor ones, are such an adrenaline rush, and I felt my heart beat quicken at the prospect of time alone with Angelo. As she left the room, Kary giggled in a high pitched, mad, impish way. Bathed in a comfortable artificiality, I congratulated myself warmly on my victorious duplicity, but not for long because the sound of her scampering down the hall was overwhelmed by a knocking at our front door. It was, all said, a fairly feeble sort of knock, almost reluctant in style, more like a tap really. It was the sort of sound made with a single knuckle, with the back of a limpish hand. Three short raps. Caught by circumstance, Kary, being almost at the door anyway, joyfully and confidently shouted "I'll get it!" and both Angelo and I twisted in our seats to see whose weak attempts at door knocking might delay our plan for the day. Lugging open the door, even though we could only see the back of her, we both saw Kary gasp and step back a couple of times in disbelief or shock or something, for there, standing outside our house with two suitcases, one on either side of his wretched and wizened looking body and an expression akin to an animal about to be put down, was Clive.

XXXII

Despite my comparative naivety, I knew what I needed to do when James left me back at the cottage. I felt utterly drained of all emotion, except to say I was glad to be away from James' house, glad to be released from the prison of cheerfulness the situation perpetuated and keener than I could have ever imagined not to be forced into the same sorry situation myself, at any cost.

The cottage wasn't as cold as I expected it to be, even though the fire had long since gone out. I switched on a lamp in the living room and forty watts of light flickered weakly, shedding a feeble glow over nearby furniture, accentuating steadily accumulating dust and general detritus which floated in the damp air as if there was nothing much else to do. I plugged in the phone charger and connected it to the mobile phone which shone greenly. And then I hesitated. My original plan to call the Doctor, to ask for her help suddenly seemed inadequate, silly somehow. She had, after all, dumped me here in Devon, by myself. Dawn was right, I needed to see a doctor, but not The Doctor. With the mobile phone gathering in power in my hand, I lifted it slowly to my ear and dialled the only other number I knew: 999.

The ambulance was remarkably quick. Only about fifteen minutes and considering it had to come from Exeter and it had to deal with those windy South Hams lanes, I was very impressed. There were two ambulance people, both men dressed in bright green, like martians. One of them had "Paramedic" written in yellow fluorescent letters on the back of his uniform, he said his name was Martin and as he led me like an invalid into the ambulance with its red plastic and its oxygen tanks, I felt an odd sense of liberation I had never felt before. I had told the emergency operator I was losing a baby – not altogether a lie, just grammatically askew. It was, afterall my intention to lose the child, I just wasn't doing it spontaneously at that moment. My hope was to convince the hospital to lose the baby for me.

Everyone, at some point in their lives, should take a ride in an ambulance. Apart from the fact that you are the most important person in the vehicle, it is not easy to get a grip on the fact that all that equipment is for you. Whatever medical treatment you need is there. And the expert is also there, holding your hand and making constant medical assessments of you – checking your pulse, your colour, your respirations. What was amazing to me was my own reaction to all this attention. I liked it. I truly believed that Martin cared. The journey to Exeter seemed too brief and Exeter itself seemed huge and bustling. I was taken into the hospital in a wheelchair, though I'm not absolutely certain why.

Martin disappeared and I was left to sit on a hard, black plastic chair in a waiting room. No one else was there and periodically nurses and other medical staff swished through without looking at me. After some time of being ignored, a middle aged woman appeared from a side room. She was wearing a white lab coat which was unfastened revealing a chunky body supported by thin legs. Her hair was short and badly dyed a yellowish blonde colour. It looked dry like straw and the unnatural yellow colour made her skin look grey and ill. In her hand she held a card and she read my name in a heavy, disinterested south western drawl without looking up. I stood up and my legs felt heavy and big from sitting for so long. Without speaking, I followed her into a small windowless, unlit room with a tall bed covered in a white sheet and beside it the only form of illumination in the room, a computer screen.

"Lie down and relax." Loose White Coat said, still without looking at me, "Lift up your top."

I obeyed, feeling the tissue and cotton sheet beneath me crunch cleanly. A clear, warm goo was squirted and still without looking at me, the woman ran a grey plastic instrument smoothly across my abdomen whilst at the same time adjusting the screen so that what it showed was just out of my vision. I felt completely comfortable. Normal in fact. I had no idea what was going on at the time. Now, of course, I know it was an ultra sound scan. It was something I should have had a long time before, but then, I had just been swept along. I watched the woman's face as she concentrated on the screen and ran the instrument across my belly. I had no idea what was going on. For what seemed like a long time, she moved the grey instrument back and forth, her expression totally neutral, concentrating on the screen whose workings and wires I could see but whose image I couldn't. Then the woman said, still without looking at me, "Has your doctor sent you?"

"Yes," I replied, not believing I was lying.

At this, she at last made eye contact with me but they were blank, blue eyes, almost fish-like, and her expression was deliberately calm, too calm, it masked a lack of concern brought about by more important things to do.

Deftly, she manoeuvred the screen round so that I could see the image. To me, it just looked like a mass of white on black; I couldn't make it out. I stared at it for a moment and then looked at the woman with the instrument and the open white coat who sat sideways, now looking directly at me.

"I'm afraid I can't find a heartbeat." She said flatly and clearly not for the first time in her career, then, pointing to the screen, she traced an outline, adding by way of explanation "Here's the foetus. As you can see, no heart beat, and it has curled right up, almost up into a ball – they do you see." As she spoke, we both looked at the image, and I could. I suppose, see what she meant. I could just make out a profile with a nose and mouth, a spine with tiny bones and fingers outspread despite the rest of the body having contracted. This was not what I had expected. I looked at the woman with the open white coat.

"It's dead." I said, not quite a question, and she nodded with what could have passed for sympathy flashing in those fish eyes. "Yes," she said, "you were quite right when you said you were losing your baby." I looked again at the screen, fascinated, and whilst I was looking, she left the room, I suppose to leave us together, to let me begin to grieve or something.

To the left of me was a large roll of blue paper towel and I tore some off and wiped my abdomen and waist then I sat up and rearranged my clothes, actually feeling quite pleased. I was pleased that this child had died, inexplicable though its demise was, pleased that I wasn't running the risk of having another Patrick, pleased not to be a mother and pleased that some attention would be lavished on me by those who knew nothing about me. The image still remained on the screen and I wondered what would happen next so I coughed loudly. On cue, the woman returned. She seemed surprised to see me standing upright and fully dressed – and fully in control. I doubt I would have been so composed had I known what was to come.

It was easy for me to avoid questions regarding "family" or "support", afterall, it's considered ok to be too upset to give too much information in situations involving dead babies. It struck me that what people, professionals, don't realise in those situations is that they make it easy for the patient to play a part, to be what they think they should be. So I played the part quite well. I managed to cry a bit and asked to be left alone. I was placed in a side room by a concerned looking young nurse and given a cup of sweet tea in a light blue tea cup. As the door was gently closed, I mopped my fake tears away with hard white hospital tissues and took a look around the room. What struck me first was the heat. I wasn't used to warmth – the open fire at the cottage seemed to provide very little and I was aware that I was beginning to sweat. Taking off my jacket, I noticed the bed. I had never seen such a well made bed in my life. It appeared to me to be totally symmetrical and the contrast of crisp white sheets, orange coverlets and puffed up white pillows seemed almost unbearably peculiar to me. Surely it was simply ornamental, if someone slept in it, or even sat on it, the whole effect would be ruined instantly. On top of the brown bedside cabinet sat a serrated plastic jug of water covered with an orange plastic top. A very clean white wash hand basin poked strangely out of the wall and two windows either side of it batted off rain and looked out over Exeter roof tops. I wondered what would happen to me next. I was viewing it as an adventure.

I suppose I was left alone for twenty minutes or so, although that's only a guess since I had no watch or any other method of knowing what time it was. Then the door opened and a different woman in an open white coat entered. She wore a stethoscope like a necklace which clicked against a hard name badge. A testimony to the speed with which she walked was the fact that I couldn't read her name as the badge flipped wildly, pinned to her white coat. Rather outrageously, I thought, she sat heavily down on the beautifully made bed, immediately causing creases and bunching of the covers to occur. She had a tired, yellow face, rather bony and angular in shape. Creases were beginning to appear at the corner of her eyes and her pale orange lips were dry and thin. Looking at her brown eyes, I wondered how much suffering they had seen, how much angst, death. A few strands of wiry brown hair strayed across her face escaping from a loose pony tail held by an elastic band at the back of her head and she shoved them away in a gesture that implied familiarity with the process with large, knobbly fingers. If I had known then what she was bracing herself to explain to me, I probably would have paid less attention to her physical appearance and more on how I would cope. Having said that, the element of surprise is such a powerful factor in the act of coping that it is possible that knowing what she was about to say might have been even worse for my psyche. What she told me was that it would not be possible to remove the dead child inside me by surgical means because the pregnancy was too advanced and that I would have to go through the process of labour in order to expel it. I stared blankly at her, trying to work out how that would work and she told me, very clinically, which was certainly the best way in the circumstances, that the labour would be chemically started using a pessary and then an intravenous drip. At first, I felt keen to get going, although I was disappointed I couldn't just go into theatre and have the foetus removed, but let me tell you, as soon as the actual process began, I wanted to die. For eight hours I battled with the most excruciating pain. I heard the howling cry of what could have been a wounded animal, but was actually me. My insides churned and cramped, contracted and strained in a way I could never have imagined would have been possible. I swore at the staff using words I had only heard on tv. Whatever was happening wasn't happening to me, I was letting it happen to someone else, but eventually, with the angular faced doctor and the young nurse peering with concern at my exposed body I felt a slithery mass plop out of me. Only then did I become aware of the dampness of my own body, of my struggling heart beat and of my rasping breath. Doctor and nurse worked quickly to remove the contents of my uterus which I had no desire to see, and when I cried the young nurse misread my tears of self-pity for sadness at the death of the child and she comforted me with her thin bare arms and her well practised phrases whilst the Doctor removed the corpse in a silver kidney dish.

That night I slept in that crisp hospital bed more deeply than I had ever before, dreaming of nothing and waking at 6 am, feeling an instant relief at what had happened, happy that I could at last go home. As far as I was concerned, all my troubles were over and there was no reason now for anyone to deny me my place back at home, no reason to believe I would give birth to a Patrick, no reason ever to return to this place. Lying in that room, listening to the city waking up and the vague hum of machinery offering some reassurance, I decided what I had to do: Having left the mobile phone at the cottage in my rush to be swept away in the ambulance, I would escape from the hospital, get myself to James' house and reveal to him what I suspected about my parentage. I would talk to James and Dawn and we would all go and speak to the Doctor, I would return home and everything would be fine. Of course, now I remember this plan, it seems adolescent and unformed, but then so was I.

XXXIII

Clive's arrival was greeted with absolute glee from Kary. She literally threw herself at him in an abreaction which involved her fat legs being curled around his hips and her arms strangling him so that he made a reactionary choking noise. There followed a loud reunionary snogging session in which both Kary and Clive seemed to be equally involved, Clive shifting his weight from foot to foot, clipping the noisy loose floor tile so that it clicked and ground against the others in an effort to keep upright. Angelo and I watched from the kitchen as the two of them, Kary and Clive, took on the form of incestuous conjoined twins. It was me who walked up to them and, with my own weight grinding against that loose floor tile, I eased Kary and Clive apart and came face to face with both of them.

"What's this?" I asked, concise as ever.

Clive looked at Kary and the view of their profiles could have been the subject of analysis of any media student: she blinking fast and nervous, mouth slightly open inviting response rather than offering it, hair unkempt; he staring widely at her, mouth tightly shut but a corona of silvery saliva – not his - outlining his mouth as if he was deliberately holding something back; both of them caught in the moment – not my place to intervene. But I did anyway.

"Don't just stand there looking at each other. Clive." I touched his arm which was beginning to shake with the exertion of holding Kary's vast weight, "Why are you here?"

The straightforwardness of my question jolted him into a response and he turned to me, his face red with embarrassment or simply straining to hold Kary.

"I've left Jane." He said, "For good."

At this, Kary squeezed his neck tighter, planting wet loud kisses on his cheek and his face broke into a stupid smile.

I was appalled.

"What?" I asked, like some sort of primary school teacher challenging a child who had offered an unacceptable excuse for P.E. "She's just had your baby." I presented this as if it was a conclusive reason for a marriage to stay intact. What Clive gave in response was an equally inadequate idea. He eased Kary down off him and she clunked heavily onto the loose floor tile. At first, I thought he might say something but he said nothing. He shrugged his narrow shoulders as best he could, given that Kary still clung on to him, and opened his dampened mouth and looked over my shoulder as if the words eluded him and he might find them if he looked for long enough, but anyway I should know what he meant, or that it was simply too complicated for mere words and I should be able to work out from his body language alone what he really meant. This seemed to be enough for Kary who whooped and swept him, not unwillingly, upstairs, leaving me with his suitcases in our hall.

We had had to endure the giggles and shenanigans of a couple of love birds which had kept us awake whilst at the same time had amused, entertained and irritated us sufficiently for me to bring the subject up. It was a Sunday morning and I could stand it no longer. Kary's cries of mock pain as she was apparently being goosed whilst walking along the hall towards the kitchen were enough to stop me from any hesitation. Busy making tea for Angelo and me and feeling grumpy at the interruption of noise, I started by asking Kary to be quiet. I knew this would not be well met but welcomed the discussion I knew it would provoke. Kary stopped dead in her tracks, followed a second or two later by Clive. I looked round at Kary who stood with a look of demonic determination which normally pre-empted a physical attack. It was my impression that she was unlikely to launch an out and out on me in the presence of Clive, so I could afford to be a little more adventurous. Casually stirring sugar into my tea cup I informed her that the noise of her voice was more irritating that morning than at any time before and really she should consider quietening down or shutting up completely. I looked at Clive and, noticing his unkempt appearance and dishevelled clothing, reminded him that he was a guest in someone else's house and should be more considerate. For a second, I thought I might have pushed it too far and Kary took half a step towards me. Bracing myself for a slap, I automatically straightened to my full height and closed my eyes. Here was the surprise: in a split second, whilst my eyes were closed, Kary had indeed prepared to defend herself in the only way she could think of at the time, but it was Clive who, simply by uttering her name, stopped her from going any further. She retreated into his arms immediately and without question and what swiftly followed – and it was literally within hours - was the announcement from Kary that she intended to move out of our house.

The episode as a whole marked a real moment of change and now I come to recount it, I realise it was this point, this decision which led to a number of significant and life changing events.

Within a week, Clive and Kary had found a house to rent. It belonged to a work colleague of Clive's, a house left by a maiden aunt to a sole nephew who had, up to that point, allowed it to begin to rot. A small, two bedroomed dwelling, its previously white rendering was tarnished with mould and invaded by ivy. It had the benefit of being detached with the nearest neighbour being on the opposite side and some way down river, and although the white glossed wooden window frames looked sound enough, the window panes had not seen cleaning products since the old woman herself had been fit enough to use them. Inside it remained typically furnished by a aging female virgin with that sort of hopeful floral combo which can be so depressing to those of us with more than just the fantasy of love to live with. Despite this, it had an enduring, loved feel and I was, despite myself, quite truthfully pleased that Kary could possibly realise her dream of fulfilment in a place I knew she would regard as charming. In fact, there was a sense that both the little house near the river and Kary's life could at last achieve their potential.

The day we, Angelo and I, went to see it, Kary and Clive had lived in the house for less than a week. It had rained overnight and the river was high and fast. Overgrown grass in the garden lay flat and pungent and as our feet sank into the muddy excuse for a walkway to the house, I was completely unaware of the effect the next few hours would have on me and our futures. If only I had known then what fate had in store.

By way of politeness, we took off our shoes before entering what was now Kary and Clive's home. What greeted us was a surprise, for there, sitting on the scattered rugs on the floor of the tiny living room, playing a computer game on a tv that looked too old to even work let alone support the technology for the latest PlayStation, was Clive's son, Harry.

Harry's reputation had beaten him to it. Kary had previously emphasised his malevolence, his tantrums, his "difficult behaviour", but what sat before us on those beaten rugs was a child of about five who's angelic face offered a milk-toothy grin by way of introduction and, utterly surprisingly to me at the time, a litany of detailed information relating to the computer game he was so keen to play. That a child so young could be so enthused, so animated, so alive, at the time baffled me. Of course, now I think about it, it is my own reaction to what is perfectly normal behaviour which should be baffling, and sitting beside him and looking at his buttery skin and ruffled blond curls, I was swept completely into his little world, asking questions to which I already knew the answers to simply elicit a response from him, simply to hear his little voice explain, simply to periodically feel his hot breath skim my face as we conspiratorially discussed computer game tactics. His mispronunciations and his emphatic instructions affected me so deeply and so shockingly that where I had previously believed the control of my emotions had been incorruptible, my barriers were now destroyed and I could only succumb to the effect. In short, this charming child forced, with all the energy I now realise only a small child can do, a cathartic change in my thinking; he released a need so deeply buried that I hadn't even known it was there. From that day on, I made sure that on the days Clive saw Harry, I saw Harry. I made excuses to go to Kary and Clive's, usually alone but always with a gift fit for a five year old boy and I was delirious to find that with each visit, Harry's face lit up and gradually, over the course of a few weeks, we transcended the emotional and lurched into a situation where Harry would, by way of greeting, run at me with such great energy, throw his arms around me and kiss me as if we had known each other for ever. We came up with silly affectionate nick-names for each other, he was my little Happy Harry and I was his "Besfrenever". That a child should name an adult seems now so fiercely pertinent as to be agonising to me. So close and exclusive was our friendship that it didn't strike me to consider what anyone else thought. As it happened, no-one thought very much, in fact Kary and Clive were both equally delighted that my babysitting allowed them even more time for themselves. In a way, all of us at the time were engrossed in our own situations. Such is human nature I suppose – but to be so engrossed in, or by, a situation is often more than a shock to the system. Getting involved with Harry changed me in a way I had previously not considered. I came to look at life in a different way. I was keener to be of help, happier to get involved. So when Kary asked if I could get something from her old room and bring it to her the next time I came, I was happy to help her. And it was partly my new-found affability which was to lead to a shock wave of realisation, changing our lives for ever.

What she asked me to find for her was insignificant in the events that followed. Without her request though, I probably wouldn't have had any need to enter her room at our house ever again. So it is that fate works. So it was that with a light heart I set about the task she had set for me. Her room was unsurprisingly musty and I opened a window before setting about my search in her room, remembering momentarily that the last time I had done this was in search of the scalpel, but putting that entirely and swiftly out of my mind. At first, I thought the task would be easy, Kary had virtually emptied the room of her belongings and what remained were pieces of furniture now almost totally bereft of contents. I gave the task ten minutes at the outside and with Harry-like enthusiasm, started opening drawers and cupboards. All were empty, but one drawer, old and swollen, seemed to be stuck. As is the technique for opening drawers in this kind of state, I set about easing one side then the other alternately, painstakingly and slowly shifting the drawer towards me using immense effort for very little reward, only to reveal that it was also empty. However, in my child-like fervour, I had, little by little, shifted the entire piece of furniture – a large four drawer oak set – a few millimetres towards me and in so doing, heard something drop to the floor behind it, something which had maybe fallen and been wedged between it and the wall. Half thinking I might have broken something, I set about retrieving whatever it was that had fallen and shoved my hand as far as I could between the furniture and the wall, unable to see what the elusive article was, but unable to squeeze my arm far enough into the small space. Becoming more inquisitive, I stood up and using all my weight heaved the heavy wooden drawers out from the wall. At first, what was there, what had fallen and now leant, half covered in cobwebs and grey dust, against the wall, looked innocuous enough. It looked like a large book of some kind. I picked it up and with the palm of my hand wiped a line of grime off the red cover to reveal a faded word in gold print: "Photos". I smiled as I anticipated what might lurk inside the covers and though I knew Angelo would disapprove, allowed my curiosity get the better of me. It was a cheap album with that sticky cellophane that, no matter how much you try, always bubbles and eventually loses its stickiness so that any photographs you try to include tend to slip out or displace. This album was no exception and as I opened the pages, photographs jostled towards the middle so I was forced to scoop them together and look at them separately. The first few pages were terrifically nostalgic: pictures of the three of us as babies in pushchairs, as toddlers with coloured toys; as teenagers, spotty and blushing at the camera. Then some photographs of landscapes – the Devon coastline and boats out at sea. Pictures of us on the beach, pictures of us gluttonously devouring ice cream, pictures that caught us chatting aimlessly, and then, at the moment when I was feeling at my warmest, at the moment when I was least expecting it, a photograph fell from the centre of the album. At first, I didn't register anything, still swimming in a haze of dopey memories and sunny days, but then, when my thoughts caught up with the rest of me (or vice versa), when my new thinking realised what fate had delivered, I dropped the album to the floor. It was a Polaroid photograph, fading, but the subject still clear. I held it with both hands, as if the physical act of doing so would help me to remember properly, would somehow magic me there, back into the picture, like rubbing the genie out of the lamp. The face that stared up at me was tanned and smiling, eyes bright and hair damp. In the background a calm sea, and further out a small boat bobbed, out of focus. James' face laughed out at me, urging me to remember, making sense of that spontaneous act, the act of a fifteen year old so many years ago. Suddenly, I remembered grabbing that old camera and taking that photograph and suddenly I was that fifteen year old again. Overcome with nostalgia, I felt the heat of my own tears before I realised I was shedding them and I let them flow without wiping them away. James. The album lay on the floor now, in a hazy bubble of blur through my tearful eyes, and in my scrabble to collect it, yet more photographs fell, more smiling faces, more embarrassed looks. And there, amongst the cultivated expressions, there was the thing that fate wanted me to find, the turning point, the crux. In amongst the glossy pictures was a hand written note written on a spiral bound note pad and pulled haphazardly out of the rest of the pad, the edge torn off. I rubbed the tears roughly from my eyes and there, a hasty hand had written in faded ball point pen "I think she knows. We ought to talk about this. Can we meet? J." In a moment, the urgency of those short sentences, the brevity of the request, the illusion of fate set the rest of the terrible events in motion.

XXXIV

My escape from the hospital was shockingly easy. I changed into my clothes, left the hospital's pyjamas behind, pulled the canular out of the vein in my hand to release myself from the intravenous drip, dressed and simply walked out. True enough, I felt a little shaky, especially my legs which were heavy and tight, but I figured this was just a reaction to the trauma. Relieved to be out of the sterility of the hospital room, my intention was to find a taxi to James' house. I could remember his address and even though I didn't have any money, I thought, like children do, that someone there would pay for me.

My mind was a jumble of ideas. Looking back now, it's not easy to rationalise, to make it sensible, but at the time, logic didn't enter into it. I just wanted to get to James and tell him my theory of our connection. At the time, I was just ticking off problems one by one, working on automatic.

Outside the hospital there were several white taxis but I had, of course, never used a taxi before and had no idea what to do. So I stood on the pavement, arms folded against the bitter cold, like the lost, lonely child that I was, watching the way that the system of taking a taxi seemed to work. How odd, now I look back, that my life hadn't ever given me the opportunity to sample everyday situations and that there I was, totally alone, waiting. As it was, I didn't have to wait long. Across the road, an old man wearing a flat cap and a green-brown overcoat raised his arthritic arm and mouthed something into the air which seemed to galvanise one of the taxi drivers into action. A taxi pulled up along side the old man, who clambered in and the car drove off. It seemed easy to me, so nervously, I crossed the road and repeated the same routine. Sure enough, I was rewarded with a similar white taxi and I clambered into the back seat. Inside, the cab smelt of a mix of sour milk, cigarette smoke and sickly lavender and I felt my empty stomach lurch for a second. The driver watched as I sat down, twisting his body familiarly. "Where to?" He sounded friendly and I gave him James' address. Feeling pleased with myself, I started to relax. As soon as I sat though, my legs took on that "over-exercised" feeling and I could sense the beginning of an uncontrollable trembling deep inside my thigh muscles. A familiar ripple of cramp flushed through my insides within a moment and I felt my stomach twist in pain. I was glad to be sitting down. The driver was observing me using his mirror and his disembodied eyes gazed unblinkingly at me. I managed a smile and wondered how far we were from James' little house.

"You alright?" The driver asked.

I nodded but felt a warm rush of fluid leave me and instantly cool on my underwear.

"You sure?" He persisted in that way that adults do with children.

I nodded again, this time more vigorously and with a smile. Then, in an effort to waylay conversation, I averted my gaze to outside, concentrating on trying to look as normal as possible whilst realising with increasing anxiety that the gnawing pains in my abdomen and the wetness of my underwear was going to be out of my control fairly soon.

The driver took my hint and once we were out of the city, concentrated on navigating the narrow lanes. Meanwhile, despite the cold, I wound down the window and felt the sharp air instantly slap my face, like an abusive mother, or like Kary had done so many times.

It took longer than I imagined to get to James' house. We were held up on the way by cars from the opposite direction – those lanes weren't meant for two way traffic. When we arrived at James' house, I could see, with relief, a dim light coming from the living room. Glad that someone was in, it took me longer than I imagined to get out of the taxi, and, sliding out, I noticed a dark blood red patch on the fabric of the seat where I had been sitting. Instantly embarrassed, I told the driver I would be back in a moment and trotted up the path. Dawn answered the door quickly and, noticing the taxi blocking the lane, rushed out with her purse. Standing there at James' door watching Dawn pay the taxi driver, a tremor of agony gushed from my legs up and the last thing I remember is my knees buckling and the taste of sourness in my mouth.

I woke up in a strange bed unsure how long I had been sleeping. Floral curtains were drawn against the dimness of the night and the sound of a television or radio programme buzzed monotonously from another room.

There was still enough light to distinguish various items in the room: the flowery carpet, the light, cheap wardrobe. On the table beside me a tray contained a glass of water, some pills and a thermometer, and a bedside light. I flicked it on and blinked to accommodate the change in light. My clothes had been removed and I was wearing a pair of blue and white striped pyjamas. My face felt tight as if it had been washed with soap and beside me in the single bed was an old brown teddy bear whose beady black eyes stared heavenward. I swung my feet out of the warmth of the bed and onto the stubble of carpet, sitting for a while, scooping together reason and logic, memory and common sense to try to work out what had happened to me. My legs still ached but the pains in my abdomen had subsided a little leaving me with a feeling of emptiness and tense lightness. As I sat on the edge of someone else's bed, my movements must have been monitored, listened out for, because in an instant the sound of hasty footsteps on the stairs brought Dawn into the room. In the gloom, something in her eyes – whether it was anxiety or concern, I didn't know – made her movements jerky and she sat on the bed next to me, not touching me, back straight and jaw tensed.

"Are you alright?" It wasn't a question I expected from her. Her body language invoked a feeling that what she would say would be more like a statement. And to use such insipid vocabulary: "alright". What does it mean to be "alright" anyway? To ask such an inadequate question seemed, in the circumstances, extraordinary to me. So I hesitated, half because of surprise and half to consider how to answer. I was not "alright" as it happened. Feeling physically drained, physically exhausted and still in some pain was only part of it. I couldn't quite work out what was going on inside my own head. My thoughts were confused and there were some ideas floating around, dark and worrying which were causing me to be distracted from what I had previously thought was reality. I suppose I was what some people refer to as depressed, and not surprisingly so. But I was a fifteen year old and my developing ideals couldn't cope with such uncertainty. So I said nothing. And Dawn took my silence to mean something else and she did something and, because of my general bewilderment, I could not reciprocate: she put her arm round my shoulders and hugged me to her so tightly that I could hear her heart thudding and I could smell from her skin and her clothes that she had been cooking something starchy. My lack of response just made her squeeze me tighter and I'm sure I felt her body heave with sobs as we sat for a while in a freeze frame of sorrow, or something. More footfalls on the stairs made her release me and then Patrick arrived, standing on the threshold of the room, gawping in. Without hesitation, Dawn lifted her mood and with forced levity asked Patrick to wait downstairs. He tilted his head to one side as if trying to weigh up the situation before him. Then, with great effort, he lifted his left hand and with a stubby finger, pointed at me and grunted. Dawn strained to force out what should have been a chuckle – ever the positive mother – and turned to me. Using that nursery rhyme intonation used by nursery teachers, she said, "Oh, my goodness, yes You're wearing Patrick's pyjamas."

Patrick's face broke into a chubby grin, egged on by Dawn. Inside me, something fractured and splintered into a thousand pieces, piercing all those dark areas I had up to that point kept at bay. Suddenly my senses were in chaos, jumbled and confused, so much so that when I heard someone crying, it took me more than a couple of seconds to work out that those frantic, miserable sobs were mine.

Dawn helped me out of Patrick's pyjamas and into my freshly laundered clothes. We said nothing to each other, but every now and then I was aware that my body spasmed and jerked with immature post-crying hiccoughs and each time, Dawn mumbled something indistinguishable, more to herself than to me. Before we left the room, she looked at me with anxious eyes again and I thought she was about to say something, to tell me something, but instead she took me in her arms one last time, and embraced me wordlessly; this time I gave back as much as I received.

The narrowness of the stairs meant that Dawn had to lead the way down into the darkness of the hallway filled, rather dangerously, with Patrick's wheelchair and other equipment making us squeeze round to avoid the obstacles, walking on towards the living room. I can't remember what I expected as I followed her – probably to see James I suppose. But I certainly didn't expect what greeted me, what shook me out of my malaise and what literally threw me back into my own reality. For there, waiting for me, wearing thick coats and concerned expressions, were Angelo and the Doctor.

Angelo's hair seemed longer and he looked tired. His blue eyes were framed by the dark circles of sleeplessness and in the bright light he looked pale and thin. As soon as he saw me, his expression lightened and I rushed at him like an escaped prisoner, holding and kissing him hungrily, breathing in his skin, not quite believing he was there, feeling him respond just as keenly. The Doctor observed us with a calm disinterest and when we eventually released each other, she asked us to sit down. In the distraction of reunion, I had missed the fact that Dawn had left the room and felt all at once uncomfortable, uneasy with the situation and I clung onto Angelo like a child to its mother. In my apprehension, the silence that followed was unbearable and my worst paranoias flipped in and out of my thoughts so that within seconds I believed the Doctor was going to tell me I was to live in Devon for ever, I was to stay and fend for myself, I had better enjoy the few moments I had with Angelo because this was the last time I would ever see him, I was to live a desperate life in that cold, damp cottage for ever. I did the only thing I felt I could do at the time. I said "Take me home, please."

The last thing I remember about that bitterly cold night in Devon is watching the lights of James' house disappear into the distance as the Doctor drove, oh so carefully away, down those narrow, winding Devon lanes.

XXXV

The effect of Kary's absence from the house was telling. Our "pattern", so previously fixed and unmoving, had been unfixed and had moved. Outwardly all remained well. In fact, Kary clearly did not wish to set foot back in our house, refusing all requests adamantly. So Angelo and I quickly reformed our own patterns and routines as if, in fact, she had never been there. We were like two peas in a pod, me and Angelo. Yet something about her absence unsettled us in a way it is impossible to describe.

Remarkable as it may seem now, I didn't tell anyone or do anything about the note or photograph album I had found in Kary's room – despite instinctively knowing what the coded message meant, despite being rudely reminded of my teenage traumas. I had, as it happened, parcelled up my past into a dim corner or my mind, never to be revisited, never to be re-examined. But with the discovery of this tatty photograph and scribbled note, I knew there was only one thing I could do. The more I thought about it, the more I wondered how Kary had come to acquire this memorabilia and why she had kept it without telling us. The more I thought about it, the more I couldn't help wondering whether that missing link in the pattern could filled if only I could somehow speak to Kary and find out what she knew.

My alternate Saturdays were now spent ostensibly visiting Kary but really playing with Harry at the cottage by the river. This time, I chose to go via town, to drop in on Angelo at work and to buy Harry those sweets he liked so much. I had tucked the photograph album in my bag and my plan was clear: I would speak to Angelo first but whatever he said, I intended to tackle Kary about why she had kept the photograph of James and the note without telling us.

Town was busy despite the rain, and the cobbled mock-Victoriana of the shopping precinct felt treacherously slippery underfoot. Angelo's shop was empty of customers but its powdery warmth was instantly comforting. The old fashioned bell on the door alerted Angelo's boss who seemed to spring into action, appearing from another room, grateful, I suppose, for a customer. When he saw it was me, his expression changed from hopeful to a kind of knowing resignation and with only minute hesitation, he said, "If it's Angelo you're after, you've missed him." His voice had a brittle quality, enfeebled by age or lack of use. By comparison, my voice sounded strident, resonant somehow, "Do you know where he's gone?" The old man, by now, allowing the disappointment of lack of customers to weigh heavily on his shoulders, shook his fat grey head and said in a mumble without looking at me "There was a phone call and he said he had to leave." Then, gathering himself physically and emotionally, added, "He promised to make up the time." Instantly agitated at both the old man's priorities and Angelo's disappearance, I stepped forward, asking who the phone call was from. The old man looked at me with watery yellowed eyes and for a second I thought the expression I saw was, puzzlingly, one of fear and I realised I may have been a little abrupt in my confusion. So softening my voice and demeanour as much as possible, I added "I expect it was Kary?" The old man nodded and his mouth widened a little into what should have been a smile whilst his eyes stayed fixed and apprehensive. Overcome with guilt that this poor old man clearly felt uncomfortable with me in his shop, I leaned forward, stretching my arm over the grubby counter and touched his shoulder, conciliatory style. "Thank you." I said in what I thought was a sincere tone, but to my amazement, the old man recoiled, jerking suddenly backwards, the expression on his face changing to utter distain. His twisted lips seemed unable to form the words he wanted to say and he stood impotent and defensive, gawping stupidly. Self-preservation made me reflect his actions, and I too jerked backwards in sheer shock at his reaction. Aided by physics or gravity, common sense or self-protection, I continued to step back until I felt the cold handle of the door, twisted it and left as quickly as I could. Outside, cold air, or something, took my breath away. An urge to cry simmered dangerously inside me and that familiar constriction of the throat made me cough dryly. Despite myself, I looked back through the window into the shop. Through my own reflection, I could see him, still standing in the same spot where he now strained to scrub and clutch at the shoulder I had attempted to touch as if it were contaminated, as if, if he could have, he would have wrenched out his own arm rather than have me lay a finger on him. And his face. His face revealed a contempt that cut through the distance between us in a way that even Kary had never been able to do.

I can't explain the effect this short, shocking episode had on me, except to say that I don't remember the journey to Kary's house. My automatic reactions took me safely across roads and fields, through the woods and across the bridge, and despite being soaked through, I felt nothing but confusion and a deep nagging wretchedness that even the catharsis of crying couldn't dilute. As if fate, or something, was testing me even further, what greeted me at Kary's house was, to put it mildly, not what I had expected. The house was, first of all, quiet. Harry's usual cavorting and playing, computer games and general playfulness; Kary's usual attempts at cooking resulting in a pervasive but familiar smell; the general disorder, they were all missing. Today there was none of it. From the outside of the house, there appeared to be no-one in. My curiosity was, of course, heightened by the general uncertainty of the day and I consciously tried to order my thoughts. When there was no answer from the front door, I decided to try at the back. The earth was saturated with last night's downpour and the long grass fell limply like a carpet of green in a pathway to the back door. I could feel water seeping through my shoes and the numbness in my toes was beginning to feel painful. But as I tapped on the door at the back of the house, it opened, unlocked but somehow not particularly welcoming, more sinister really. I didn't like it, but I had to enter. Already formulating scenes in my mind as to what I might find – funny how quickly your mind works in situations like this, you imagine so much and move so little – but nothing could have prepared me for what I saw.

I should say, before I go any further, that Kary was never exactly a tidy person, so the sight of a trashed kitchen wasn't too much of a surprise. Tea cups sat half empty on the work surfaces, spilt hardening sugar punctuated the draining board and tea-brown semi circles littered the sink and kitchen table. These I would have expected of any kitchen in Kary's house, but it was something else that flicked a further switch in my mind: the particular disarray of chairs, as though someone had stood up quickly, shoving them inadvertently away, and left too quickly to reposition them; the particularly strange angle of the picture on the wall, as if someone had fallen, or been pushed against it, shoving it askew; the door, only just ajar, its plastic handle stuck pointing downwards as if pulled with such force that some mechanism was broken, leaving it limply hanging there for ever. A sense of panic crept into my subconscious, layered on top of the fear and confusion already so well established there, peculiarly leaving me with a bitter sense of bizarre clarity of thought. Tuning out of my own self-absorption for a second, I became aware of the rumble of voices from another room. With blatant nerve, I grabbed for the broken door handle and strode purposefully towards the living room, hearing the voices rumble more loudly as I did and becoming more aware that the voices belonged to Angelo and Kary.

The living room door was firmly closed and required me to force it open – the damp, I suppose, had expanded the wood – so that I half stumbled both into the room and the conversation. Although I expected to see Angelo and Kary, I did not expect to be so surprised, and what I saw filled me with such disbelief, such shock that I was frozen in the moment, my poor brain unable to comprehend any further surprises. Now I am aware that you may be expecting me to reveal that I discovered Angelo and Kary in a passionate clinch, him with his beautiful, perfect body, naked and blushing, she yielding to him, hungry and possessive. This would have been a reasonable assumption, and one which, in the short distance between the kitchen and the living room, I had also explored. In truth, I was expecting just that, to see Angelo and Kary together. I could fully imagine what the scenario would be, how I would react, what I would say and, to be honest, I had already forgiven Angelo even before entering the room. Such is "love" I suppose. My cognitive preparation, however, was not enough for the reality of the situation. This is what I saw: Angelo and Kary were sitting on the sofa. Angelo's arm was protectively and tightly around Kary's shoulder and she nestled her head into his neck, like a child. Both were fully clothed and both looked up at me as I arrived. In recognition, Angelo's face softened and smiled at me within a micro second, but it was Kary, Kary whose eyes were red and swollen from crying, whose neck was patterned with big red blotches, whose tee-shirt was torn at the sleeve, it was Kary who I stared at in total, complete disbelief for as she slowly lifted her head from Angelo's shoulder, as she came into clear focus through my tear-clouded eyes, I saw that her head had been completely shaved of all hair – eyebrows, eyelashes, everything. All gone. Irregular bumps and bulges on her skull had obviously been nicked leaving seeping, bloody wounds all over her head. With her swollen eyes and sallow, mournful expression, she looked like a victim of nuclear fall out or like a hybrid animal. I was, I have to say, instantly repulsed. She looked obscene. The lack of facial hair alone gave her a monstrous expression, like an experiment gone wrong, and as I looked at her, a rivulet of blood from a wound on her head dribbled down her face and into her eye, turning it pink red and eerily dead looking. I did the only thing I could. Fighting against the swirling nausea in my stomach, I walked over to her and embraced her. So there we were, the three of us linked together by something we knew nothing about, with absolutely no idea how or why this situation had happened. I don't know how long we sat there, scrunched-up uncomfortably on the hard sofa, but I do know that though we were closer then than we had ever been, the hard cover of the photograph album tucked into my bag, now dug painfully into my thigh as Kary's weight pushed it against me.

It took a while for me to become aware that dark strands of Kary's hair lay in a spiky mess in her lap. Sobs that shuddered through her body displaced it so that some scattered on the floor by our feet and some fell and stuck to the material of my trousers and on Angelo's thigh. It also took me a while to realise that in her right hand, held tightly in her fleshy white fingers, whose finger nails were painfully and nervously bitten short, was the sharp silver blade of a scalpel, yet even this knowledge did not move us and we sat, unmoving and wordless until darkness fell and the sound of the river rising against torrential rain jolted us back to our own different truth.

It was Kary who moved first. She released herself from us, stood up and clicked on a lamp which threw a white light into the room. Standing, pathetic and miserable, in front of us, the light making her look a peculiar shade of yellow, she said she would make us some tea and left for the kitchen. As soon as she had left, Angelo embraced me, kissing my face and neck with a forceful vigour and for the first time ever, it was me who retreated from him. As though he could read my mind, Angelo sat back and, with a clarity I had not expected, explained in a whisper what had happened.

"I can't tell you how pleased I am you came. I received a phone call from Clive at the shop. He said he was leaving Kary. Finally, once and for all, he was going. He said he intended to return to Jane. She had forgiven him. He wanted to be with her and the children. Obviously, I was astounded, and angry, and sorry for poor Kary, I said, How is she? He said, that's why I'm calling you. She's not taken the news well, she's gone a bit mad. He said she was screaming and calling him terrible names, tearing her clothes – you know what she's capable of. He said she suddenly appeared with the scalpel," and here, Angelo paused and looked at me knowingly, "of course, Clive remembered all too well about the scalpel." He paused again, "But at first I think he thought she might hurt him, that she might stab him or something, but she just stood in front of him and dragged the thing through her hair, like she was making him watch her do something so incredibly, well, weird, that he would realise how upset or mad he had made her or something." Here he stopped and looked reflectively about the room. "Obviously, he tried to stop her, but she just went even madder and in the end, he just had to stand and watch as she…" and here he paused again, but this time more to search for words than for dramatic effect, "…as she literally scalped herself. Clive just watched in disbelief I think, and then, he just left." Another pause "I don't think he'll be coming back. She's freaked him out good and proper this time." He sat up and flicked some stray hairs away from his trousers. "I just came right over and she was sitting here, crying hysterically. I could hear her from outside."

When he finished talking, I sat, as people do, absorbing what I had heard, trying to cut through the layers of meaning, the complex tangle that, far from being straightened out, was in fact becoming more complicated as time wore on. I tracked back through it all: Kary's situation, Angelo coming out to her, Angelo's boss' reaction to me, the photograph album, James, Devon, the way the three of us lived, the relationship we had with each other. When Kary came back into the room – how odd she looked with her bald, injured head, carrying with her a tray of tea, looking more like a manikin or a discarded broken doll than a human being – the three of us talked in a way we had never done before. Numbed by the events of the day, Kary's reaction to the photograph album was anaesthetised, over-calm. She said she had, in her kleptomaniac days, taken to rifling through everyone's handbags, including the Doctor's, and this was where she had found the photograph of James and the note, which, to her, had meant nothing except something else to steal, as simple as that.

As we sat, together again on the sofa, talking about our past and our present, unpacking a parcel of issues we had until then taken for granted, there seemed only one answer: the Doctor must know more than she had said, or more than we had asked her to tell us. Now was the time we needed to know who we were.

Outside, night fell quickly but as I took a minute to look out of the window at the never ending rain, and the river flushing away like time, I caught a glimpse of my face reflected through the darkness in the grimy window pane and could clearly see smudges on my cheeks and chin, tainted areas which gave my face a look of unsuccessful disguise. Curious, I rubbed the skin of my face with my hand and inspected it quickly. Blood, some still wet, was smeared on my finger tips, browny-red.

Kary's blood .

XXXVI

The rain fell all night. None of us slept. We sat in Kary's living room, drinking tea until we could stand it no more, talking about what we should do and, for the first time it seemed, listening to what each other was saying. It was the clocks, not the daylight that told us it was morning. In a way, cocooned in that little house, formulating ideas so openly, we all felt a security unlike any we had felt before so that the mere thought of leaving, for any reason at all, seemed dangerous in the extreme. So it was with great trepidation that we set out to see the Doctor.

Fierce, pointed raindrops hit us at an acute angle, permeating our clothes and our shoes and our skin, chilling us to the bone in minutes. We walked, head down, like soldiers, battling against the elements. Nobody spoke. No-one broke the silence because everything had been said. And as we walked, it occurred to me that never, since we had lived apart from the Doctor, since we had all lived as adults in our house with the tiled hall and the unkempt bathroom and the cosy kitchen, had we visited the Doctor together. True, we had all been to see her, but separately, and even then we were ushered into a kind of "consulting" room, a room that was clean, tidy and

211

warm, a room with easy chairs, fresh flowers and a vague smell of lavender, a room with a window overlooking a perfectly landscaped garden. Walking through the slimy-wet streets, greyed with cloud, feet slipping every now and then on the increasing chemical concoctions on the pavement, bit by bit the feeling of anticipation was concentrated into a much deeper feeling of indignation, of a need to know fuelled by a growing rage.

It took us more than thirty minutes to walk to the Doctor's house. When we arrived, numb with freezing cold, we stood looking up at the building as if waiting for an instruction from a higher being or as if each of us was expecting one of the others to do something dramatic. Kary was the first to speak.

"She's not in." She said flatly, blinking against the persistent rain, "Her car's not here."

The Doctor had always seemed to us to be a creature of habit, and Kary was right, her car was not there. In the place she always parked her car, bluey-green patches of leaked oil changed shape and dimension like a screen saver on the tarmac road. Our plan apparently scuppered, we stood on the roadside, sedated for a moment by both the elements and the situation until without warning, Kary shoved Angelo hard so that he stumbled forwards.

"Come on!" She yelled, the old Kary back with us, eyes pin-pricked by squinting, "Let's go round the back of the house."

Angelo and I didn't object. We simply followed Kary as she strode purposefully across the drive, the hood of her coat now blown off by a bitter wind revealing, literally in broad daylight, the obscenity of her large, wounded head, looking for all she was worth like a new born baby. As we had suspected, the immaculate back garden was empty. In preparation for the rain, tasteful garden furniture had been tilted and arranged so as to retain optimum dryness. Having previously only viewed the garden from the inside of the house, I was surprised at its size and privacy. Tall poplar trees guarded three edges and ivy crawled up along side them to fill in any gaps. There was a palpable sense of exclusion which bordered, for me, on an uncomfortable claustrophobia. Whilst I surveyed the grounds, Kary was busy trying every door and window handle in an effort to get into the house. Just after I heard Angelo's plaintive attempt to abort the proceedings, there was a shattering smash. Startled and jolted back to reality, the sight of Kary, having broken a glass window pane, fiddling with total concentration to reach an internal handle was utterly comic in its stupidity. She worked with great haste and with absolutely no help from Angelo or me and within a few seconds, the window was open. Kary turned to look at us, her face pinched with determination, droplets of rain running down off her lumpy head. Somewhere in the distance a police siren sounded and it was this sound that prompted us to move. Quickly grabbing Kary and shoving her, bald head first through the broken window frame, Angelo and I clambered roughly and without abandon through and into the consulting room we knew so well.

An intense smell of lavender was the first to assault our senses, immediately kicking off memories and associations with long consultations sessions in this room, consultations sessions which now it seemed tackled nothing as far as we were concerned. They were suddenly meaningless. But that smell of lavender instantly resulted in a feeling of absolute guilt at what we had done, at what we had thought. Angelo hung his damp beautiful head in shame and I know if Kary had told him to, we would have left the Doctor's house there and then, but she didn't. Far from appearing guilty, Kary seemed revived by the familiarity of the room, empowered by it and without a word, she marched out of the door and down the long hall. She was drenched and left child-like smudgy footprints on the Doctor's otherwise spotless carpet. Angelo and I followed her, aware that her small dumpy frame would probably not be able to stand too much more of the assault course into which we had placed each other. I don't know what I hoped for. Adrenaline was beginning to cloud my thinking and I had to steal myself to retrieve control.

"Kary," I heard myself say, "Where are you going?"

When she didn't respond, when she kept walking deafly down the hallway, I hurried to catch her and touched her shoulder in an effort to slow her down so that I could try to work out what the plan was. As soon as she felt my touch, she stopped, breathing heavily through her nose in agitation. I repeated my question, aware that in our cumulative panic, we had lost track of what we had come here for. We came to see the Doctor; she wasn't in. What could we possibly do now? Kary's body relaxed and in letting go, she seemed to slump, both physically and mentally. I could feel the panic welling up inside me, the last thing we needed now was for Kary to go into one of her "giving up" phases. Without thinking, I took hold of her fat shoulders, and pulled her to me, embracing her tightly. Stubble on her head grated against my chin and I had to field off an initial surge of disgust or pity or something indefinable. She didn't cry, as she would have in the past, she didn't shout, instead she let me hold her, and I did. Moments passed, and in those moments I became aware that I was so accustomed to the pattern of Kary's behaviour, that we were all innately aware of each other, we had absolutely no choice but to find out why. We owed it to each other. Behind us, Angelo's breathing evened out and I could feel it on my neck – so close was he to us without touching us. And then I noticed something. Looking back now, I don't know why it seemed significant, maybe heightened emotion fuels suspicion or paranoia, or maybe one sense intensifies another in certain situations, but what I noticed was a particular smell. It wasn't a strong smell – far from it in fact, but it was an insidious one, a sickly undercurrent of an aroma, and I found myself releasing my grip on Kary as if relieving my brain of the burden of the sense of touch would help it concentrate more on the sense of smell. Sniffing the air like some sort of animal scouting for its prey, I turned around slowly in the hall, identifying at once that the smell had a harsh antiseptic quality similar to the atmospheric odour of a hospital. By now becoming hypnotised by this strange sensory overload, I started walking, zombie-like, towards an open door which seemed to lead to some stairs down to a cellar area. Without considering the consequences, I pushed the door and, followed by Kary and Angelo, descended into the darkness down narrow steps. There was no handrail and as I felt along the cold flaking paintwork on the brick wall, my hand fell upon an old-fashioned round light switch which fizzed as I flicked it and which activated a buzzing fluorescent light in the area below. At the bottom of the steps was another door to the right slightly ajar and, taking a one look at Kary and Angelo who had followed me closely, I walked into the room in the cellar.

I had been right about the fluorescent light. One single strip light cast a flickering whiteness over the small, rectangular, windowless room. It should have been a cellar, somewhere to store wine or to stack memorabilia. It should have been a chilly storage room, extra space, a study maybe. It might have been awash with cardboard boxes, a lair for spiders. It might have contained the electricity or gas meters to be visited periodically to check on readings and to tut-tut about impending bills. It could have been, but it wasn't. This cellar was none of those things. This cellar was, in fact, a fully equipped, clean laboratory. There were no spiders here, no cardboard boxes, no meters, no mess. Surfaces were perfectly white, and even without scientific confirmation, we just knew everything was completely clean and hygienic.

Down there, where the air was thick with the smell of disinfectant, and coloured charts bedecked the walls, where vials, test-tubes and pipettes were strategically placed here and there, down there the three of us stood.

Almost simultaneously Angelo, Kary and I wordlessly started opening cupboards, cabinets and drawers, looking through their contents. Then I noticed a filing cabinet, white, like everything else so it was camouflaged amongst the blandness, each of its three drawers labelled with a simple handwritten card. The top drawer, labelled "X" slid easily and soundlessly open and was full of buff coloured folders, each dated, from 2006 to the present day. For no particular reason, I scooped out a folder dated 2021 – ten years ago – and flicked through the white unlined pages full of frenzied and corrected handwritten notes. Through the crossings-out, one entry read "Subject confirmed as pregnant" and what followed was a remarkably candid account of my miscarriage in Devon: how I had telephoned the Doctor, how I had been transported to Devon and left "to deal with the situation". I snapped the folder shut and replaced it quickly into its place in the filing cabinet. Feeling a rising, queasy panic, I realised that behind me, Angelo and Kary were still rifling through cabinets and cupboards, oblivious to my discovery, and I gawped at the filing cabinet, amazed at the dawning realisation that my whole life could be chronicled in that drawer. Beneath it was a drawer marked "A" and one marked "K". Now, remember that mine was marked "X". Somehow the recognition that I had not been afforded a name, only an "X" made me half madly curious, half terrified at what I might discover. I was mesmerised and, still looking at the cabinet as if it was the answer to all our questions, murmured "Angelo, Kary. Come and see this." Both of them scurried to me. "What is it?" Kary asked.

"It's our lives, in a filing cabinet." It sounded as preposterous as it actually was but it was the only way I could think of explaining.

So with Angelo leaning apparently casually against the pristine counter, one slender leg crossed over the over as if he was simply scanning a magazine and Kary now seated without grace in the corner on the floor, with only the top of her bald head clearly visible as one by one, entry by entry, in silence we read the files. Enclosed in closely written, sometimes illegible handwritten text in buff coloured folders were the records of the events of our lives converted into statistics, graphs, experiments, situations, reactions. They were all there. Our lives objectified. And we read every word, every figure without comment, dancing with our own respective devils, with only the buzz of artificial light to help us.

Our consumption of the information was voracious as we desperately scanned the words for meaning. So much were we absorbed by the facts in the folders that footsteps on the stairs went unnoticed, and it was only when the Doctor arrived in the laboratory that we lifted our heads out of our past.

"So," she said flatly after some time of watching us, "You've found it."

She moved a little further into the room and suddenly the dynamics were changed, so that Angelo stood to her left, I to her right and Kary now remained gracelessly on the floor behind her.

"I'm glad." The Doctor was smiling now, a sort of ambiguous tranquillised smile, a smile that could have shown any number of emotions but didn't. Without warning, she turned to Angelo and said "Don't you have any questions?" Her face, illuminated from overhead, looked old; her pale eyes, sunken and encircled by dark shadows, three deep lines etched into her forehead. Angelo stared dumbly back at her, like a reprimanded child. For a second, I thought he might indulge her, I thought he might ask a simple question just to placate her, but he didn't. The Doctor's face wrinkled into another grin. "Oh, my dear, dear little Angelo." And her voice seemed to catch on what might have been affection but she didn't move any closer to him. Turning to me, her eyes fixed onto mine and as her smile faded, she asked me if I had a question. And I asked it. A question we had curiously and bizarrely never even thought, so were we programmed. And it tumbled from my lips as if I was hypnotised, and asking it left me feeling like a rag doll whose stuffing was escaping from a tear, whose innards, without care, would, little by little, leak and never be replaced, leaving me empty, bare, wounded. Again, the Doctor smiled wanly "At last you have asked the right question." And she sighed a long, heavy sigh, and, like a rag doll herself, emptied herself, as if she had been longing to forever. "At last, you ask the question that young children ask. I thought when you became pregnant ten years ago that I might be faced with this one, but no. You were too self absorbed to think. It's all recorded if you want to read it. Everything is here." Here she turned her head to survey the laboratory, and then, looking benignly at me, she continued: "I call this room my chameleon room. I can create anything I want here. I can change things, alter things, change people. You want the truth about where you came from and the answer is simple: you came from me." Here she hesitated and her eyes widened slightly, glazed over slightly and we kept listening. "There has never been any need, or time in my life for a relationship in the conventional sense. I'm too much of a creature of habit and I was busy studying, working. Lots of people want children and it was my life's work to help them, to be above the scientific law that chooses who shall and who shan't. But you three." She snapped back to us. "Well, to explain, you need to know a little science to understand the logic." Here the Doctor moved uncomfortably and was that a patina of sweat on her forehead? She continued: "The lease was up on my premises in Devon and I had to move on. I spent some time experimenting and researching. The problem with the treatment I was performing was that the incidence of certain birth defects - syndromes and mental retardation and the like was likely to cause an issue in the future. Not just for me you understand, but for the birth industry in general. I had disposed of literally hundreds of frozen embryos belonging to those couples I had tried to help, but there were still a number of these embryos that I didn't know what to do with. It seemed such a shame to discard them, and I did, afterall have a need to meet my own biological commitments." Biological commitments. Birth industry. So typical of her to use such functional language, it somehow detached her from the act she was about to describe. She went on: "So, partly by way of experimentation, I implanted several spare embryos into myself." There comes a time in every conversation when we begin to speed-think, to pre-empt what will come next. That moment had now arrived. Pausing very briefly so as not to give any one of us a chance to interject, the Doctor continued. "They, the eggs that is, came from a variety of sources and parentage but they would otherwise have been simply destroyed. It seemed such a complete waste to me. I had, after all, been so busy with my work, I could feel time slipping away. At the time I felt as if it was some sort of payback. Fortunately, I tested positively pregnant straight away – some of my patients hadn't been so lucky." She hesitated again and, as if searching to recapture the memory, gazed over my head in bleary recollection and it was difficult to tell whether what we saw was maternal or professional pride. "And the result? Well it was you. Three different children from three different sets of biological parents with me as the birth mother." Allowing the idea to settle, she paused, tilting her head slightly to the left as if weighing up my response and when she could detect none from me, her face hardened and her voice quietened and, directing her comments first to me, and then to Angelo in turn, she continued. "You were my experiments."

Stunned into confirmed silence, I felt my jaw slacken. Noticing this, the Doctor took a sympathetic step towards me. "At the time there had been only been 20 odd thousand babies born as a result of this treatment worldwide. The available data was broadly reassuring for the short-term health of babies like you, but information was sketchy, and people needed to know about long-term health issues. As a longitudinal study, you have helped medical science press forward in leaps and bounds." In disbelief, my rag-doll stuffing continued to pour out and I heard my own voice, high and tight, echo round that horrible little room "Your experiments?" I choked back a sob of disgust.

"Yes," she was calm and in opposite reaction to her, I could feel only utter confusion and horror at what I was hearing. "You didn't even give me a name." I tore my voice out in tatters but she stepped closer still.

"The incidence of mental retardation was high," she motioned towards Angelo without actually looking at him, "but it is my work on chromosomal analysis that has been hailed as a complete success, which means that people like Kary can be helped in the future – indeed without Kary, I'd be a complete failure."

Behind her, I saw Kary, still seated in a heap on the floor, jolt a little. Unaware, the Doctor continued addressing me as if the other two were not there. "And you, you were such a weak little thing, I didn't know if you'd survive." Another step closer. "I know it was hard for you in Devon. It had to be, don't you see?" I could feel my anger, my disgust, a sickening revulsion rising from deep inside me. The thought of her procurement of a relationship between Angelo and me revolted me enough, but the idea that my child was – would have been - just another experiment in the so-called advancement of science stunned me to the very core. The sense of over-stimulation, the amount and depth of information she was giving me sent me into a temporary confusion, but then, as I re-ran what she had told me in my head in order to make some sort of sense of it, a painful clarity took over, an awful precision of thought struck me: Clive's on/off relationship with poor Kary took on a new obscenity, the appalled reaction of Angelo's boss mirrored my own; the idea that the sheer loathing I felt for myself at that moment was the feeling I, we, invoked in others. How many people knew?

"Your work has been a complete success?" I asked, trembling. She nodded as if she felt a penny had dropped and that I had suddenly understood everything, and in a way I had. "So," I continued, allowing my thoughts to complete themselves in the sound of simple words, "Everyone knows about us." With a final step towards, me the Doctor nodded, like a criminal caught out, like the person who had put the cat in the bag, the knave who stole the tarts. And she placed her hand on my arm in confirmation of our connection, a sudden knowing smile spreading across her face – it reminded me of when we were younger and Angelo and I had first got together, but there was something different now, something strained and odd about her face. Inexplicably and suddenly, before my face, her expression was changing. Her eyes no longer focussed, and to test her I moved my head slightly to one side to see if she continued looking at me. She didn't. Instead, in an instant, her face lightened into an expression of surprise and then crumpled into one of agonising pain. Behind her, Kary stood firm, hands now on hips, and as the Doctor released her grip on me and collapsed forward like a broken doll, the scalpel still fixed in a place between her shoulder blades, I was sure I saw a glimmer of a satisfied smile on Kary's lips.

Escaping blood quickly saturated the Doctor's white blouse and leaked into a gloopy pool onto the floor where she lay. Some spread outwards towards my shoe and I stepped hastily away in an effort not to let it reach me. We could all hear the Doctor's laboured breathing, but it was Angelo who spoke first.

"Oh my God Kary. What have you done?" His voice sounded strangled with a yodelling, pre-pubescent quality about it that I hadn't heard before. Kary glared at him with blazing, mad eyes, and as the bubbling, frothy sound of the Doctor's breath begun to abate, Kary turned on her heels and retreated back up the stairs, leaving me with Angelo and the body of the Doctor – our "mother" - in the laboratory.

I was absolutely convinced that we had to resolve matters. We were too close, we were a family afterall, we relied on each other, we knew our patterns of behaviour. Without each other the triangle would fall apart and I knew that. Without each other we were nothing. We needed each other. We couldn't live without each other. But it seemed long after we heard the front door bang shut upstairs that Angelo turned to me and said "What shall we do?"

The answer seemed simple to me. "We'll go after her," I said, "I think I know where she'll be heading." And, stepping over the now unmoving body of the Doctor, we switched off the flickering light, closed the door and left.

I don't remember much about the weather or who said what to whom on the journey back to the house by the river, except to say that Angelo was concerned that we find Kary at all costs. By the time we arrived at the river however, we were drenched. The little house, unlit, looked empty, derelict almost, from outside but Angelo insisted on going in. I decided that this time, I knew better. This time, I would find Kary. I would be responsible for saving her.

It had been raining and the light was beginning to fail behind the sad looking deciduous trees whose aging leaves were deserting them. The impression was one of brownness, of dourness, of cold. Out of the corner of my eye I saw a figure, small and naked. Falling. Falling from the muddy river bank. What must have been a split second shot. Very white skin, almost torpedo shaped body, stubby feet seemingly clamped together at the ankle and arms raised high above the dome-like, hairless head. Not a graceful pose, more like a child's drawing of a fat ballerina. But instantly recognisable.

I knew she would be here.

Those reluctant links between us were, after all, impossible to break.

Printed in the United Kingdom by
Lightning Source UK Ltd., Milton Keynes
136876UK00001B/51/P